HENRY AND THE NIGHT SKY AND OTHER STORIES

Joseph F. Persinger

Kin
An A

D1502852

This anthology consists of works of fiction. Names, characters, and incidents are products of the author's imagination and are not to be construed as real. Any resemblance to actual events, organizations, or persons, living or dead, is entirely coincidental.

HENRY AND THE NIGHT SKY AND OTHER STORIES
© 2021 by Joseph F. Persinger. All rights reserved. Printed in the United States of America.

ISBN: 9798726712826
Imprint: Independently published

Contents

✳ ✳ ✳

The Dreamer

The boy walked along the two-lane blacktop road that stretched away in a long, sweeping curve leading into town. His white sneakers made soft plopping sounds in the talcum-like dust that lay alongside the asphalt and coated the weeds and tall grass along the road. He wore khaki cotton trousers bleached almost white by repeated washings and a pale blue short-sleeved cotton shirt with the sleeves carefully rolled up an extra inch in the style of the day. His light blond hair was cut in a "flat top" carefully waxed to maintain its shape.

He rarely wore a shirt of any other color because one of the girls in his class had told him he should always wear blue to match his eyes. She said he should never wear green because it would clash with his eyes. He did not have any green shirts.

As he walked he could see the courthouse tower rising above the trees in the distance, illuminated by the July sun, which was rapidly dropping behind the hills in the west. His sense of excitement began to increase as he left the highway and made his way along a residential street toward the courthouse square. As he grew near he could hear the sounds of music, shouts and laughter, and various rumbling and clacking noises, and he walked even faster.

The carnival was in town.

The event was advertised as the annual soldiers' and sailors' homecoming and reunion by the veterans' groups which sponsored it, but to the townspeople it was simply "the carnival." It was a highlight of the summer, second only to the county fair which came a month later.

As he rounded a corner the town square came into view, and he saw the merry-go-round in its usual spot on the southwest corner, its brightly painted horses rising and falling to the oom-pah sounds of its mechanical calliope. A small group of parents stood watching as their children enjoyed the ride.

The boy made one quick lap around the square as if to reassure himself that all the other attractions were in their rightful places. The carnival changed very little from year to year — you could count on the rock-o-planes, the tilt-a-whirl, the Ferris wheel, and the octopus all returning to their usual spots. In between were tents offering various games — the baseball toss, basketball, ring toss — all offering three chances for a quarter with huge stuffed animals as top prizes.

At one point he spotted some of his friends from school, hurrying through the crowd, laughing and pushing and punching each other, but he did not join them. On this night he preferred to be on his own.

When he reached the main thoroughfare that formed the fourth side of the square, he saw that the town marshal was directing traffic, helping crowds of pedestrians cross the busy street. As he crossed to the corner drugstore, leaving the carnival behind, it occurred to the boy that it was like leaving a fantasy and stepping back into the real world.

A breath of cool air greeted him as he entered the drugstore, and he stopped for a moment. The spicy fragrance of root beer syrup, musty vitamin/medicinal smells, and the leathery pungency of adhesive tape wafted over him. He took a seat on one of the stools at the soda fountain counter. A tall, slender girl was washing glassware in a sink behind the counter.

"Hi, Freddy," she said, smiling. "Can I get you something?"

He returned the smile. "Yeah," he said. "A chocolate Coke."

Nothing more was said while she filled the glass with ice and cola, shot a quick spurt of chocolate syrup into it, and placed it on the counter.

"Are you going to the carnival later?" he asked.

"Oh, sure. I suppose," she said. "I have to work until eight."

She returned to her dishwashing, and the boy sat and drank his Coke. When he had finished, he stood, placed some coins on the counter, and said, "Okay. Well. I'll see you later then, Sarah."

The girl looked up, smiled, and then turned back to her work.

The crowd around the square was growing, and darkness was falling now, throwing the colored lights, banners, and garish posters of the carnival into bright relief. The boy joined the flow of people moving along the sidewalk between the edge of Main Street and the cast iron fence that surrounded the courthouse yard.

Once again he passed the merry-go-round, now even more dazzling as its hundreds of electric light bulbs glowed against the darkening sky, illuminating elaborate gilt ornamentation and mirrored panels that circled the top of the carousel. The music played on, the mechanical mallet pounded the big bass drum, and long lines formed at the ticket booth, parents struggling to hold on to children who tugged and pulled impatiently, their eyes fixed on the magical machine.

"We've got a winner here!" one of the barkers yelled.

The boy turned and saw one of the senior boys from the high school swaggering away from the basketball booth, grinning widely and holding aloft a huge blue and white plush teddy bear. The boy envied him, but he knew his chances of winning anything were "slim and none," as his father would say.

He walked on, past the rock-o-planes and the

octopus and the booth where some of the older boys and young men lined up to show their strength by swinging a huge mallet trying to ring the bell at the top of a post painted to register their prowess from "sissy" to "he-man." Occasionally one of them would be successful, and the sound of the bell would ring out across the square.

He passed the Presbyterian Church, where tables with white tablecloths had been set up on the lawn, and ladies of the church were serving homemade ice cream. On the opposite side of the street, a barker was urging people to enter the "fun house" for a scary walk through dark, claustrophobic mazes punctuated with startling buzzers, horns, flashing lights, and unexpected blasts of air, and mirrors that distorted your reflection into bizarre shapes.

"Let's go if you're going," the barker chanted. "It's show time!"

The boy left the fun house behind and had just turned the corner onto the north side of the square when he heard "Pssst! Hey, kid! C'mere a minute!"

He turned and saw it was the barker in charge of another carnival game, a tough-looking fellow but only a few years older than he was.

"You ever try this game, kid?" the barker asked.

The boy shook his head.

"Well, I'll tell you what I'm gonna do," the barker said, glancing around as if he were preparing to share a great secret. "I'm gonna give you a free one."

He held three baseballs in his right hand, and he thrust them at the boy.

"Come on," he said. "It won't cost you anything. This one's on me!"

The boy reluctantly took the balls.

"All you have to do is knock over the three milk bottles and you win your choice," the barker said, pointing out the brightly colored stuffed animals hanging overhead.

The milk bottles, which looked as if they were made of lead, were stacked in a pyramid on a small wooden platform.

The boy stared at the target, drew back and threw the first ball. It hit nothing but the back of the tent. He blushed furiously, hoping no one in the crowd had seen.

"Whoa-ho!" the barker cried. "Take it easy there, Ace. You can do it. You've still got two more chances."

The second throw rocked the top bottle. It didn't fall, but the final attempt brought it down.

"Hey, you're good at this, Jack!" the barker exclaimed. He held out three more baseballs. "You're gettin' warmed up now. Take down all three, and you can have your choice, pick out any prize you want. Your girlfriend would like to have one of these big ol' teddy bears, wouldn't she?"

The boy hung back. "I'd better not," he protested.

"Hey, it's just a quarter, kid. You can do it."

"No, really —"

"Hey, man — I gave you a free one. You got to practice once; least you can do is try one for real."

"I can't." The boy shook his head. "I have to meet someone. I have to go." He turned and started off through the crowd.

"Well, you can just go to hell!" the barker yelled after him. As he turned back to his booth he muttered, "Last of the big time spenders there, folks."

The boy pushed blindly through the crowd, his ears burning, eyes smarting as he searched his mind for a scathing retort and found none. "I didn't ask to play your stupid game!" he thought.

When he looked up again he had already reached the corner where the Ferris wheel stood. He took his money from his pocket and counted it. He could ride the Ferris wheel for a quarter and still have enough money for two more rides and two Cokes. He bought a ticket, got in line, and soon the ride operator, a stringy-haired man with tattoos all over his forearms, motioned for him to come up the ramp. He had a seat all to himself.

He took a deep breath as the wheel jerked into motion and he felt himself rising through the warm night air, rocking gently, both hands gripping the safety bar in front of him. Up and up the wheel carried him and then stopped while more riders boarded below. The boy looked out over the street where men, women, and children scurried about, hurrying this way and that. He could see the roofs of the drugstore and the savings and loan building across the street, and to his right the appliance store on the corner and the furniture store beyond. The drugstore was closed now, its windows dark. At his left loomed the tops of the massive maple trees in the courthouse lawn. The bright lights of the Ferris wheel turned the green leaves a ghostly silver against the backdrop of black sky.

As the wheel turned, lifting him up, over, and down, his eyes scanned the endless stream of people moving around the square, some traveling in one direction, others the opposite way. The motion of the wheel combined with the churning of the crowd made everything seem unreal, the boy thought, like a dream. And that made him think of what his teacher had said in the spring when he graduated from sixth grade.

"You're a dreamer, Freddy," he had said, "not a doer."

The boy had said nothing at the time but he felt the comment was unfair and resented it. After all, he thought, he was among the top students in his class and got A's on almost all his assignments and class projects. He was involved in sports, and band, and choir — if that wasn't *doing*, what was?

The memory made him uncomfortable, and he forced himself to turn his attention back to the sights and sounds in the street below. He tried unsuccessfully to focus on a particular face amid the swirling mass.

Soon the ride was over, the Ferris wheel operator freed him from his seat, and he walked back down the ramp to the street. He was facing the fish stand, which had occupied that same corner during carnival week for as long as he could remember. The same thin-faced man worked in the stand every year, too, taking orders and calling out to the cook, "Swim one!" or "Swim two!" and the cook would drop more breaded fish filets into the vat of boiling grease. The cooking area was surrounded by glass, and the cook kept a supply of fried fish piled up against the end window to attract passersby. Two large cylindrical glass containers — one holding lemonade containing slices of fresh lemon and one holding orangeade with slices of orange — also drew attention. The thought of a hot fish sandwich and a cold cup of lemonade was tempting, but the boy knew he would need all his money later.

Once again he joined the stream, but this time walked in the opposite direction around the square, giving the baseball toss a wide berth as he hurried by. The noise level was increasing as the night wore on with the screams and squeals of people on the wilder rides added to the music, the barkers' cries, and the clatter of machinery. On he walked, weaving his way through the throng, jostling, being jostled, constantly looking ahead, scanning the faces of those approaching him.

And then he saw her, moving toward him in the crowd. It was the moment he had dreamed of. He started toward her but then stopped abruptly. She was with someone else, hanging on his arm, laughing and talking; her hair thrown back, her eyes sparkling.

The boy turned, walked quickly the other way around the square, and started down the long road home.

Luther's Love

Morning light was barely peeking over the forested ridge behind Luther's cabin as he came out and crossed to his battered old pickup truck. He was a short, pudgy man with a ruddy complexion and thinning hair. He wore faded bib overalls, a plaid shirt, and heavy work shoes.

He fired up the Ford and headed down the long lane leading to the county road that would take him into town. It was October, and the wooded hills that dominated the area were ablaze with color — the gold of hickory, orange of maple, and the red and purple of sassafras, sumac, and black gum.

As he drove along the winding two-lane road, Luther thought about how much his life had changed in the past year. He had lived alone in that little house at the foot of the hills since his parents died years before, and everyone assumed he would be a lifelong bachelor. Then, about six months ago, without a word to anyone, he went off to the city and returned three weeks later with a wife.

Maggie was tall and full-figured with long, curly blonde hair. Her arrival was the talk of the town. Some said she seemed nice enough. Others dismissed her as clumsy and coarse. And no one could imagine how Luther had persuaded her to marry him.

"I know what they say behind my back," Luther muttered to himself as he drove. "'Luther's too old and ugly to get a pretty wife like Maggie . . . Maybe he *paid* her to come out here . . . He's prob'ly gone crazy out there in them hills.' Well, they're just jealous, that's all. I see men lookin' at her, wishin' they were in my shoes. Just plain old jealousy!"

Ten minutes later he drove across the railroad tracks at the edge of town and pulled into a parking space in front of the grain elevator and feed store. A bell jangled as he entered the store. Bags of ground corn and chicken mash stacked along one wall gave the place a sweet, musty smell. There was a long glass-front counter displaying curry combs, brushes, and other products used to groom and care for livestock. One wall held shelves filled with bottles of flea spray, canisters of bug dust for vegetable gardens, and various creams and ointments to treat horses or cattle.

The proprietor, a thin man in jeans and chambray work shirt, entered from a back room. He adjusted his glasses.

"Mornin' Luther! How ya doin?"

"Mornin', Cecil. I'm alright." Luther crossed to the counter.

"And how's that pretty wife of yours?" Cecil asked, grinning.

Luther's chin jutted forward. "What you mean by that?"

Cecil's grin vanished. "Why, I didn't mean nothin', Luther. I was just trying to make conversation, that's all."

Luther frowned. "Well, Maggie's just fine. You don't need to be troublin' yourself about her. My wife's just fine."

Cecil cleared his throat. "Well, uh . . . that's great. So, what can I get for you, Luther?"

"Fifty pounds of cracked corn."

Cecil crossed to the stack and picked up a large brown paper sack tied at the top with a piece of heavy twine. He carried it around the end of the counter and sat it down next to Luther. As he moved back behind the counter he said, "Oh, I almost forgot! That stuff you ordered to get rid of the groundhogs came in. I've got it right here."

He bent down behind the counter and came up holding a small brown glass bottle with a black cap. He placed it on the counter and leaned forward conspiratorially.

"I have to tell you, Luther. I'm not licensed to sell this, and I know you're not certified to use it. I'd appreciate it if you don't tell anyone where you got it."

"I won't. Don't worry about that."

"You just sprinkle a few drops of this on some shelled corn and drop it down the groundhog hole. It'll get rid of them."

"Okay."

"But listen to me, Luther!" Cecil held the bottle up in front of Luther's face. "This is powerful stuff. The salesman said if a person ingested just a few drops, it would kill them within minutes."

"What's that mean — ingested?"

"It means don't *swallow* any of it, Luther! Don't get it on your hands, don't get it on your food. That stuff'll kill you!"

"Well, I'm not stupid, Cecil," Luther snapped. He slipped the little bottle into the pocket of his overalls. With a grunt, he picked up the bag of corn and hoisted it over his shoulder.

"Just put it on my bill," he said as he crossed to the door. Cecil, slowly shaking his head, watched him go.

Back at his house, Luther parked the truck and went into a small shed at the end of the gravel driveway. He took the bottle from his pocket and placed it on a shelf. From another shelf he took down a small blue pasteboard box labeled "Federal Ammunition. Game Load. Twelve-Gauge, Number Five shot."

He took a half dozen of the dark red shells, capped with brass, and slipped all but one into his pocket. Then he picked up a twelve-gauge, single-barrel shotgun that was resting in a corner and flipped the release lever to break open the breech. He slipped in the shell, snapped the weapon shut, and checked the safety.

Luther crossed to the house and entered through the back door. Balancing the shotgun loosely in his right hand, he quietly moved down the hallway to the kitchen and stopped in the doorway. Maggie was at the sink, washing dishes, her back to Luther. He stood watching her for several seconds. Then, sensing his presence, she turned with a startled shriek. One hand flew to her mouth, her eyes wide. Then, seeing Luther, she recovered.

"Oh, Luther! You 'bout scared me to death!" she scolded.

"Sorry. Didn't mean to," he mumbled.

"I didn't hear you come in. What are you doin' with that shotgun?"

He looked down as if he'd forgotten it was in his hand. "Oh. I thought I'd do a little huntin'. Maybe get a couple of squirrels before dinner."

Maggie knew that by "dinner," Luther meant lunch. And the evening meal was "supper." Coming from the city to the country, the difference in terminology had confused her at first.

"Well, put that gun down, and I'll pour you some coffee," she said.

Luther leaned the shotgun in a corner and took a seat at the kitchen table. Maggie brought him a cup of coffee and one for herself, and sat opposite him.

"How was everything in town?" she asked.

"Oh, same as always. Just went to the feed store, got some corn for the chickens."

"Cecil doing okay?"

"Fine, I guess. Why? What do you care?"

"Same as I'd care about anybody, Luther. Just neighborly."

"He wanted to know about you, too."

"Well, that was nice of him. To remember. Don't you think?"

"I guess."

They sat in silence, sipping their coffee. Finally, Luther asked, "What've you been doin' this mornin'?"

Maggie's face brightened. "Oh, I've been sewing. It's something really special — I'm so excited! It's not done yet, but maybe I can show it to you when you get back after while. It's a surprise."

"Well," Luther said, rising. "Prob'ly should get goin' before it gets too hot. I'll be back in time for dinner." He picked up the shotgun and left.

An old logging trail starting behind Luther's barn led up the wooded hill or "knob," as the locals would say. The path was covered in a thick layer of previous years' leaf litter, and more brightly colored autumn leaves were floating down from the mix of mature hardwood trees on either side. As he continued up the gradual slope, Luther let the shotgun balance loosely in his right hand. Occasionally he looked up into the leafy canopies, squinting against the sunlight that filtered through.

16

Several minutes later, he paused at the top of the ridge and looked out across range upon range of forested hills that marched across the landscape. The logging path continued along the crest of this ridge, dipped, and then rose to the top of the next hill, continuing in that way for several miles. The trail across the state-owned property had not been used for logging for several years, and greenbriars, weeds, and tree seedlings were beginning to encroach on the track.

Luther walked a few more yards along the ridge and then turned off the path, moving into the woods and down the slope of the hill as quietly as he could. At the base of a large white oak tree, he turned and sat on the ground with his back against the trunk and the shotgun across his lap. Directly in front of him, and father down the slope, was a huge shagbark hickory tree — one the hunter knew well.

He sat in silence, concentrating fiercely on the upper branches of the hickory. A mosquito made a zinging noise near his left ear, but he ignored it.

Then he heard a faint but familiar sound as bits of hickory nut shell dropped from high in the tree, pattering lightly down through the foliage to the ground. Luther leaned forward and to one side, trying to peer through the leaves to locate the squirrel that was dropping the cuttings.

A twig snapped, breaking his concentration. A few yards to his right, a younger man was edging toward the hickory tree. He held a .22 caliber rifle and, as

Luther watched, he steadied himself against a tree trunk, aimed and fired. A gray squirrel dropped down through the branches and plopped softly onto the forest floor.

"Nice shot, Tom," Luther said quietly.

Startled, the young man spun around.

"Damn, Luther! I didn't see you there." Then, as he grasped what had happened, he added, "Hey, did you have your eye on that squirrel? You're welcome to it. I didn't know there was anyone around."

"Nah, that's alright," Luther said, getting to his feet. "You shot it fair and square. There's plenty more where that one came from."

"Well, if you're sure." Tom moved down the slope to pick up the squirrel and then followed Luther back to the ridge top. Luther stood with his feet apart and the shotgun cradled in his arms, waiting as Tom approached.

"Been out here long?" Luther asked.

"Nah, half an hour maybe." Tom looked around and added, "Wish we'd get some rain. Lot easier to move through the woods without makin' noise when the ground and the leaves are wet."

Luther didn't respond, and the silence grew heavy until Tom blurted, "Well, gosh! Luther! Imagine runnin' into you out here. How you been doin'?"

"I'm doin' just fine."

"Good, good." Tom nodded emphatically. "Say, how's that wife of yours?"

"She's doing' fine, too." Luther frowned. "Why? You like my wife, do you?"

"Well, sure," Tom stammered. "I mean, I don't really know her, but she seems nice. Real nice lady. And talented, too — I saw that quilt she sewed for the women's club raffle. Real nice."

Tom glanced around again nervously. Luther remained silent.

"In fact," Tom continued, "I wanted to talk to her about that. I stopped by your place a while back. You weren't there, though."

Luther leaned forward ever so slightly and thrust out his chin. "Oh, I know you were there. I know. People think old Luther's not too smart, but I don't miss much. I know what's going on. I'm not as dumb as people around here think."

Tom began edging backwards and gestured toward the opposite edge of the ridge.

"Well, hey, Luther. Uh, I'd better get goin'. Think I'll just cut straight down the knob here and go out through Heller's orchard. Quicker that way. I need to be gettin' home. Be noon 'fore we know it. Good to see you, though."

Tom turned and starting walking across the crest of the ridge, away from the trail toward the dropoff that would take him down through the forest. As he walked away, Luther raised the shotgun and aimed it squarely at the back of Tom's head. He held the gun steady until the younger man reached the edge of the slope and then fired.

The swarm of lead shot struck Tom's skull with the force of a sledgehammer and threw him forward. His lifeless body slithered face down over the thick layer of waxy dead leaves, coming to rest against the base of a scrubby black oak tree. Echoes of the shotgun's roar rumbled and reverberated through the hills and valleys.

Luther stepped up to the edge of the ridge and looked down the hillside at the body and the puddle of blood that was quickly forming around Tom's head. Holding the gun in his left hand, he shook his right fist and yelled, "Try to steal *my* wife, you sonofabitch!"

Luther picked up the dead squirrel that had fallen from Tom's hand and started down the trail to his house. As the adrenalin in his system wore off, his confidence began to fade. He went a few yards farther and then stumbled over to a moss-covered log and sat down, leaning the shotgun against the log next to him. He sat with his elbows on his knees, his hands clasped in front of him, his head down. His mind was racing.

Scenes came rushing back: Maggie and Tom in the yard behind the cabin, talking and laughing. Maggie's head thrown back, her blond curls bobbing in the sunlight, bringing her hands together in delight. They didn't know Luther was in the barn, watching, growing more and more agitated. He couldn't make out what they were saying, but their obvious happiness together stunned him, made it hard to catch his breath. "No, Maggie, no!" he thought.

Their banter seemed to go on endlessly. But then she reached out and *hugged* Tom, pulling him close. Luther felt as if his heart would simply stop beating. The pain was unbearable.

The embrace ended with both of them smiling happily. Tom walked around the house to his truck and left. Maggie went back into the house, and Luther stood there in the barn, crushed, trembling, his world turned upside down.

He replayed it all in his mind, sitting there in the woods, but the smell of burnt gunpowder that lingered around the shotgun brought him back to the present. The elation he had felt in pulling the trigger had turned to despair.

"They'll find Tom's body," he thought, "maybe in just a few days. The sheriff and his men will come and take me away. It'll all come out, everyone will know. And I'll never be with her again. It's all over."

He was angry with Maggie for betraying him, and yet he still loved her. "I couldn't do to her what I did to Tom," he thought. "I couldn't stand to see her all bloody and broken like that."

Luther looked up into the trees, as if an answer could be hidden in the branches. "We could run away somewhere together," he thought, and felt a flutter of hope, but it quickly vanished. "They'd find us in no time," he realized, "with their computers and the internet and all that. And besides, she'd want to know why we needed to leave — she'd want a good reason.

But if I told her about Tom she'd hate me. She wouldn't go with me."

Time passed as he sat there, desperately trying to think of a way out — for himself, and for Maggie, too. A light breeze rippled through the tree canopies high above, and autumn leaves drifted down, making a barely audible rustling sound as they came to rest on the forest floor and brushed against the log. Songbirds chirped, and off in the distance crows cawed.

At last, Luther rose, picked up the shotgun and started down the trail toward his barn and cabin. He went directly to the shed, where he put the remaining shotgun shells back in the box and stood the weapon in the corner. He took the little brown bottle off the shelf and slipped it into his pocket, then headed for the house.

"Oh, good — you're back," Maggie said as he entered the kitchen. "I'm just making sandwiches for lunch, if that's okay. Would you like coffee?"

"Yeah, I would," Luther said as he took his seat at the table.

She poured two cups of coffee and placed one in front of Luther and one at her place. As she turned away and busied herself with the sandwiches, Luther removed the bottle from his pocket and, keeping it below the table, removed the cap. He reached quickly across the table and spilled several drops of the syrupy liquid into Maggie's cup. She still had not turned, so he poured a similar amount into his own coffee, capped the bottle and put it back in his pocket.

"Here you go," Maggie said, turning and placing a ham sandwich in front of Luther. When she turned back to finish preparing her own, Luther gave both cups a quick stir.

He closed his eyes for a moment. Then picked up his cup with both hands, raised it to his lips and took a sip. Then another, and another. The poison had no discernable taste.

Maggie brought her plate to the table and took a seat. "I hope you like your sandwich," she said. "That's honey ham — I think it's really good. And I put lettuce and mayonnaise on it — just like uptown." She took a bite of hers.

"Better drink your coffee 'fore it gets cold," Luther mumbled. He raised his cup and took another sip as if to demonstrate.

Maggie picked up her cup, but before it reached her lips she put it down and started to rise. "Oh, I can't wait any more," she said excitedly. "I've got to show you something!"

"But your coffee —"

"I'll be right back," she said over her shoulder as she hurried to the back room. And in a moment she was back, her outstretched arms holding a swath of white satin.

Luther pointed to her coffee cup. "You need to drink —"

But Maggie exclaimed, "This is what I've been working on. It's not near done yet, but I can't keep it to myself any longer."

Luther stared at the white cloth, but he was having trouble focusing. It was all he could do to raise his hand and point weakly to her cup. "Your coffee —" he whispered.

But Maggie rambled on. "You know Tom Blevins who lives over by the water company?"

Luther's eyes widened at the mention of Tom's name.

"Well, Maggie continued, "he stopped by here a while back and told me him and that Fleenor girl from down our road are gonna get married! I think that's so sweet! And here's the surprise part: they want *me* to make her wedding dress. Isn't that wonderful?" She held up the dress at arm's length and looked from it to Luther and back again.

"I've never sewn anything this fancy before, but it's starting to take shape, and I think it's going to be fine."

Luther moaned, struggling to grasp what she was saying.

"I think it's so romantic," Maggie went on. "I just hope she'll be even half as happy with Tom as I've been here with you!"

Luther tried to clear his head by shaking it from side to side, but it fell forward, his chin resting on his chest.

Maggie draped the wedding dress across the back of a chair. When she turned back to Luther she frowned.

"Luther, are you alright? Luther?"

She placed her hands on the table and leaned across to look more closely at his face.

"Luther? Luther! Whatever is the matter with you?"

She started around the table toward him.

"Luther? Can't you hear me? Luther!"

She touched his shoulder.

"Luther! Answer me! Luther!"

Roller Rink Ruby

T he high school gym was decorated with twisted ribbons of crepe paper in the school colors — black and gold. On the stage at one end of the room a disc jockey was playing hits from the nineteen-sixties, and hanging above him was a large banner proclaiming "Welcome, Class of 1965 — 50th Anniversary Reunion."

Classmates and spouses mingled and chatted in small groups, some holding a wine glass or bottle of beer.

As the DJ played the old instrumental tune, "Sleep Walk," five of the men gathered around a table. They all had gray hair, a couple were going bald, one had a full beard, and another sported a goatee.

The one with the long gray beard called out, "Mike! Hey, how you doin'?" They shook hands.

"Oh, I'm great, Dick. Everything okay with you?"

"Yeah, I'm fine — just getting older every day. But I guess that beats the alternative, right?"

Mike looked around at the other classmates in the group. "Wasn't sure I wanted to do this, but then I thought — fifty years! Wow! Didn't seem right to skip it."

Another classmate, mostly bald, exclaimed, "Say, look at Ron. He's still got his senior cords!"

Another added, "And he can still *get in* them — that's what's amazing!"

Ron stepped forward, looking down at his pale yellow corduroy trousers decorated with various colorful cartoon characters, slogans and sayings. "What comes from living right, I guess," he said with a grin. "George, Bruce — good to see you."

"You too, Ron," George said. "By the way, you remember what happened to Mary Lou because of her senior cord skirt?"

"No, I don't think so."

"Well, the theme for our prom was 'A Night in Paradise,' and because of where she had that printed on her skirt Mr. Duncan thought it meant something dirty and made her go home and change!"

"No kidding? Wow! Good thing he didn't read *my* cords that carefully!"

"Seems to me Mike and Dick spent most of their summers trying to peek into those slumber parties at Mary Lou's house," Bruce recalled. "It's a wonder you both didn't get arrested."

"Oh, they knew we were there — don't kid yourself!" Mike said. "Besides, we didn't see anything — just a bunch of girls in baggy pajamas with their hair up in curlers!"

"This old building is full of memories isn't it?" Ron mused, looking around. "Remember the time we let those chickens loose in the science lab on Friday night and left them all weekend? What a mess!"

"What a smell!" George exclaimed as they all laughed.

"We should go check it out," Ron suggested. "I bet you can still smell it."

"Nah, I think they tore down that whole part of the building," Dick said. "The stench finally got the best of them, I guess."

"You remember whose idea that prank was?" Mike asked and then answered his own question. "Tom Hoover. He was always getting us into some kind of trouble. Our class instigator."

"Yeah, he wasn't too smart, was he?" George recalled.

"That's right," Ron said. "He got held back two terms — Truman and Eisenhower."

They all laughed, and then there was a brief pause in the conversation. Finally George said, "Then there was the time we all carried Mr. Duncan's little Volkswagen up to the second floor landing and left it in front of that big half-circle window. You could see it from the street!" This brought more laughter. "Don't remember how they got it back down."

As if on cue, they all pulled out chairs and sat at a

round banquet table. Another classmate, Doug, joined them. "Hi, guys. Say, Dick, you still play the guitar?"

"Oh, I get it out and strum a little sometimes. Just for my own amusement, as they say. For a while we had a little band at my church, but that fizzled out, so I don't play much now.

"Well," Mike said, "I don't want to get all sentimental or anything — at least until I've had a few more beers — but, honestly, I'd have to say the time we spent trying to put our little rock band together was the most fun I had in high school. It really was."

"I know what you mean," George said. "Not that *The TrueTones* were that great — that's for sure — but when you got into a song and everything was meshing just right, it was like nothing else I've ever experienced."

"It's true," Ron said. "A lot of my high school memories are connected to that band in one way or another."

The lights seemed to dim slightly as the DJ played "Yesterday" by The Beatles . . .

In October, 1964, the trees around the high school were decked out in gold and bronze, and with every breeze — still pleasantly warm — a few leaves would flutter down to the grass below. After the final bell, students streamed from the building. Country kids headed for the big yellow buses lined up across the street, while the town kids walked off in all directions.

One of the girls was strolling along the shady sidewalk, carrying a couple of books. She had glossy black shoulder-length hair, which made her bright blue eyes even more startling. She wore a black jumper over a red blouse with cream-colored polka dots.

Mike ran to catch up with her, calling, "Cathy! Hey, Cathy! Wait up!"

She stopped and turned. "Oh, hi, Mike. What's up?"

"Oh, nothing. Well, that is — I just wanted to talk to you."

She waited for him to continue, but when he didn't, she asked, "Is something wrong?"

"No — no, no! Everything's fine. I was on my way to practice some songs with the guys, and I just thought — well ... " He paused, but then the words poured out rapidly: "Look, you and I have been going out for a while now — movies and skating parties, Coke dances — and it's been nice. I guess I'm trying to say that I like you a lot, but I know you still go out with Tom Hoover sometimes. Still, I was hoping maybe, that is, if you feel the same way, that we could just go out with each other from now on — not date other people, I mean."

After a long pause, Cathy said, "Mike, are you asking me to go steady?

"Yeah, that's it. I've got my class ring here." He fumbled in the pocket of his jeans and finally pulled out the ring. "I even bought a little gold chain," he added, holding it up, "if you want to wear it like a necklace. I mean, if you want to wear it at all." As he suddenly realized she may say no, his eyes widened in alarm. "But if you don't —"

Cathy, reaching out to touch his hand, said, smiling, "I'd love to wear your ring, Mike. Tom Hoover's just a friend, a buddy. I don't feel the same way about him that I do about you. I don't want to date anyone else — I just wasn't sure you felt the same way."

"Wow! So this is it, then — we're going steady. This is fantastic!"

He smiled happily as she took the ring and placed it on the chain, then placed the chain around her neck. Mike embraced her, awkwardly at first, and then kissed her softly on the lips.

"I guess this means you're my girl now," he said.

"Well, don't forget," she said, "it also means you're my guy!"

The next afternoon George was at home, sitting on the couch, strumming his guitar when Mike burst through the front door.

"George! George! We've got a big problem! Where's Ron?"

"He's in the bathroom . . . teasing his chest hair."

"Well, tell him to leave the poor thing alone! And get him out here!"

George ran down the hallway and returned a minute later, pulling Ron along with him.

"Okay, now. Calm down, Mike! What's going on?"

"*The TrueTones* are supposed to play at the Moose

Lodge tomorrow night — our first big show outside of school —"

"We know, we know!" George said impatiently.

"What's wrong?" Ron demanded.

"Doug's dad sold the bass!"

"What? He can't do that!"

"Well, technically, Ron, it's his dad's bass, so I guess he can. He has already. It's gone!"

They all pondered the situation for a moment.

"Maybe if we all go over and plead with his dad he'll buy it back," George suggested.

"Doug already tried that. No luck."

"Maybe if we all chipped in we could buy a bass," Ron offered.

"If we all chipped in we couldn't buy a hamburger! We're not even getting paid for this Moose thing — just a chance to play for a real audience."

"Do we even know anyone else in town who owns an upright bass?" Ron asked.

"Nope."

"Maybe one of the music stores would have one we could rent."

"We don't have any rent money either, dummy!"

As they all tried to think of a solution, Mike suddenly exclaimed, "I've got it! I know what we can do!"

"What?" George asked, obviously skeptical.

"Yeah, how are you going to fix this?" Ron added.

"We'll borrow the bass from the band room at school."

"Oh-oh! I don't think that's a good idea, Mike."

"We can ask," Ron said, "but I bet Mr. Shelton will say no."

"So? We won't ask!"

"We just take it?" George said nervously. "Oh, boy! I really don't know about that — we could get in all kinds of trouble! They might think we stole it!"

"They could kick us out of school! We wouldn't get to graduate!" Ron added.

"We'll have it back in the band room Monday morning — nobody will even miss it over the weekend," Mike said.

George stood with his hands in his pockets, shaking his head dejectedly. "I just don't know . . . ."

"This Moose Lodge dance is a *big deal*, fellas!" Mike argued. "A chance for us to play for real people, not just a few students! A chance for the whole town to get to know our music! We can't just let it slip away!"

Getting no more comments from Ron or George, Mike continued: "Come on, you guys! Don't be such weenies! If anything goes wrong, I'll say it was all my idea."

"It *is* all your idea!" George said.

"Come on, let's go!" Mike headed for the door, and the two reluctant conspirators shuffled along behind him.

The next night, *The TrueTones* were in rare form playing for the annual dance at Moose Lodge No. 321.

Adults and teens danced to the songs they played, including "My Guy," "Everybody Loves Somebody," and a new Beatles ballad, "If I Fell."

Halfway through the evening their full-out rendition of "Twist and Shout" drew sustained applause from the audience, but their elation was short-lived when Mr. Shelton, the high school band director, emerged from the crowd and strolled in front of the bandstand.

"Nice bass, boys!" he said sarcastically.

"Mr. Shelton!" Ron blurted. "I didn't know you were a Moose!"

The teacher shook his head in disapproval. "Just have it back at school — all in one piece — before classes start Monday morning," he said before walking away.

The dancers probably didn't notice that the next song was a little shaky starting out, but *The TrueTones* had survived their big night.

The school year rolled along uneventfully until just after Christmas break, when Ron approached the other band members as they were having lunch in the cafeteria.

"Hey, guys!" he said excitedly. "You'll never guess what happened to me!"

Poking at his plate of Spanish rice, Mike muttered, "No, probably not."

"Hey, that's not fair. I'd be interested if *you* had big news."

"Yeah, that's true," George admitted. "Okay. What's the big deal, Lucille?"

"I've met the most beautiful girl in the world! I'm gonna ask her out."

George and Mike exchanged eye rolls before George said, "Uh, I hate to remind you, Ron, but you were voted 'least likely to succeed' when it comes to women."

"Not this time, George. This hot babe is gonna be the love of my life."

"So where'd you meet this angel?" Mike asked.

"Well, I didn't exactly meet her — yet. I saw her Sunday afternoon at the roller rink. She's incredible! She has red hair and green eyes. And a pony tail. And she was gliding around that arena — *backwards*! — like she didn't have a care in the world — and she was filing her nails at the same time!"

As he described her, Ron pantomimed skating backwards while filing his nails. "And those jeans! She was wearing jeans, and they looked like they were painted on. And her figure — whoa-ho-ho! Boys, I'm in love!"

"Did you even get her name?" George asked.

"Her name is Ruby, same as my mom."

"Let's see," George said, frowning as if in deep thought. "Her name is Ruby. You met her at the roller rink. I think there's a song in there somewhere! You could call it 'Roller Rink Ruby'!"

"Okay, I get it, you're all just looking for a laugh," Ron said. "Nobody's taking this seriously."

"But you didn't even talk to her?" Mike persisted.

"Not this time."

"Why not?"

"Well, there's this guy . . . ."

"She already has a boyfriend?"

"I don't know if he's really her boyfriend. He just sort of hangs around. He rides a motorcycle, and sometimes he just cruises around the parking lot. He wears one of those leather jackets, like Marlon Brando."

"Does he have a name?" George asked.

"Uh, they call him Spike."

"He rides a motorcycle? And his name is *Spike*?" Mike shook his head in disbelief.

"Yeah, someone said it was a Harley something-or-other. I don't know anything about motorcycles."

"Yeah, and you don't know anything about women either," George said, laughing. "Are you really going to ask her out?"

"Next time I see her at the rink I'll walk right up to her and tell her how I feel. It'll be love at first sight. Maybe I'll ask her to go to a movie with me at the Stardust."

"Right," Mike said. "A drive-in movie in your dad's sexy Nash Rambler station wagon. That'll get her excited."

"There's no time like the present, Mike. You know what they say in Latin class: 'Carpe Diem'."

"Yep. Grab that fish!"

"Well, if you're absolutely sure you want to do this," George said. "It's your funeral."

"Yeah, the band will miss you," Mike added. "Would you like to be cremated or just dumped in a shallow grave out at the forestry?"

Ron started to walk away but then turned back to face his pals. "You guys are crazy. You're just jealous. She's the girl of my dreams, and nothing's going to stop me!" He turned and stormed out of the cafeteria.

After a moment, George said, "Spike's going to kill him, isn't he?"

"Yep," Mike agreed. "Ain't love grand!"

The roller rink was located on the outskirts of town, just across the river. Skating parties were a popular form of entertainment for all ages, but especially for youth organizations, including church groups, 4-H clubs, Boy Scouts, and Girl Scouts. The rest of the time there was open skating for anyone who could pay the nominal admission fee. There were rental skates for those who didn't have their own.

It was a sunny but cold day, and Ron was waiting just outside the entrance to the building, pacing and frequently checking his watch. He was also keeping an eye on the parking lot but had seen no sign of Spike.

Then Ruby came out. She was wearing a winter coat trimmed with fur over jeans and a shirt — just as Ron had described to his friends. She paused to slip on a pair of wool gloves.

Then, as she walked on by, Ron called out, "Hey there . . . ."

She turned. "Hello? Are you talking to me?"

"Yes. I, uh — I've been seeing you around the roller rink here and I've been admiring your — ah, your skating. That's really something — the way you skate backwards and do your nails and all that!"

"Oh, yeah?" She gave him a closer look. "Well, I've seen you around."

"Really?"

"Oh, yeah," she said, grinning. "I wouldn't miss a cute guy like you . . . with those Paul Newman eyes!"

Ron replied, "Really? Well, I did try to talk to you once, but you were kind of busy, and that guy, Spike, was hanging around, and I didn't know . . . ."

"Well, we won't be seeing Spike for a while."

"Oh?"

"Yeah, he's going to be out of the picture for three to five years." She paused. "Maybe 18 months with good behavior."

"Oh, I see." Feeling more emboldened, Ron said, "So, well, you're not going steady or something then?"

"With Spike? Oh, no. I like *nice* guys. Are you a nice guy?"

"Yeah! Well, that is, I like to think so."

"So what's your name?"

"I'm Ron. And I know your name — it's Ruby, same as my mom."

"Is that a fact?" She smiled warmly. "Well, I'm happy to know you, Ron. So what's up? Were you out here waiting for me?"

"Yeah." Now he's suddenly afraid she's going to be angry with him. "I've been wanting to talk to you for a while. But the right time never seemed to come along."

"So what did you want to talk about? Anything in particular?"

Ron looked down and shook his head. "I wanted to ask you something, but now I see it's probably too crazy. You don't even know me yet." He paused. "But don't say no right away — at least think about it for a second or two."

"I don't even know what the question is — you haven't asked me." A smile teased at the corners of her mouth as if she were enjoying his discomfort.

"I know. Well, I've been thinking — that is, hoping. What I mean is, I've been wondering if you would consider maybe going to the senior prom with me."

She studied him for a moment and then said decisively, "I think that's really nice, Ron. I think I'd love to go to the prom with you."

"That's okay," Ron said, starting to walk away. "I didn't mean to bother you — What?" He turned back to Ruby. "Did you say you'd like to go? To the prom? With me?"

"That's what I said, Ron. Because you're a nice guy. I can tell. So we're going to the prom!"

She took his arm, and they walked off toward town.

Spring arrived with billows of white dogwood blossoms interspersed with redbud trees along Walnut Street leading up the hill to the town park. On an unseasonably warm evening, Cathy and Mike were sitting on a park bench, kissing. As Mike's hand slowly moved down from her shoulder toward her breast, she suddenly seized his wrist and pushed his hand out away from her.

"No! We're not going to start that," she said sternly.

"Oh, Cathy! I'm sorry," Mike said, blushing. "I just thought — We've been going steady for a while now. I thought maybe it was time to — you know . . . ."

"I told you when we started going out: I'm not that kind of girl. Anyway, my mom says it's a slippery slope."

"I don't mean we should go all the way or anything," Mike cajoled. "Just . . . *part* of the way."

Cathy shook her head. "My mom says it's a slippery slope. One thing leads to another, and the next thing you know the girl is sliding right on in to the maternity ward." She made a sliding motion with her hand. "And the boy is nowhere to be found!"

"Aw, Cathy. You know I'm not like that. I'll always be around."

"No. No, you won't. Not really." She looked down at her hands, folded in her lap. "Graduation's coming up, and you'll be going off to college in September. I've got another whole year of high school. Who knows where you'll be by then?"

"Can't we worry about all that later?"

"No. I've been giving it a lot of thought. You need to be free this summer — to have fun before you go away to college. And besides . . . Well, Tom Hoover's been asking me out again, and Sheila told me you've been spending a lot of time with Melanie Stover." She flashed a dark look in his direction.

"But she's not —"

"I'm sorry, Mike, but I don't think we should go steady any more." She stood and held out his ring and chain.

Rising from the bench, Mike blurted, "But you know I love you, Cathy!"

"I know you think you do," she said, smiling sadly. "I like you, Mike — you're a nice guy. But this is for the best. We'll always be friends."

Reluctantly, Mike accepted the ring. Cathy gave him a quick peck on the cheek, turned and started back down the hill. Watching her go, he called out softly, "Cathy!" As she disappeared into the distance, he returned to the bench and sat with his face in his hands.

The next afternoon Ron was on his way to school when Mike came running after him. "Ron! Wait up!" he shouted.

Ron stopped and turned. "Whoa! What's the deal? You look like you just ran a mile."

"Well, this couldn't wait. We've got a big problem!"

"What, again? Why do you always show up with bad news?"

"I dunno. Just lucky, I guess."

"So what's wrong this time?"

"It's kind of like before — with the bass — only a lot worse!"

"Are you going to tell me, or just keep me guessing?"

Mike took a deep breath. "George is in jail!"

"What? You've gotta be kidding. George? He wouldn't do anything that would land him in jail! You sure it's not Dick?"

"No, it's George. And, strictly speaking, he didn't do anything wrong . . . not really, but the sheriff doesn't know that."

"This is *déjà vu* all over again! We're supposed to play for a big party at your brother's fraternity tonight, and you're telling me our piano player's in jail?"

"I know! And we were going to use his uncle's farm truck to haul the piano to the college."

Ron shook his head dejectedly. "Now we got no piano, no truck, and no piano player."

"I know . . . screwed again!"

"But why is he in jail? What happened?"

"Well. You know how George is kind of clueless? Well, he was walking home last night, and Tom Hoover and that bunch pulled up in a car and asked him if he wanted a ride and, of course, not having any sense, he got in. They rode around for a while and ended up out by the fairgrounds . . . ."

Ron finished the sentence. "Drag racing."

"Yep. Next thing you know the cops swoop in from all sides, round everybody up, and haul them off to jail. All kinds of charges — everything from illegal speed contests to criminal mischief for painting a starting line on a state highway."

"But George wasn't actually doing any of those things, right? Just in the wrong place at the wrong time. Like always."

"That's about it. What're we going to do?"

"You'll have to talk to the sheriff, Mike. Explain what really happened. If he wasn't involved they have to let him go."

"Oh, no," Mike said. "I'm not talking to the sheriff. No way." He paused. "But there *is* someone else I could talk to." He turned to walk away but then added: "Don't cancel the IU show — not yet. I think maybe we can work this out!"

Mike ran off toward the school. Ron shrugged and then resumed his walk in the same direction.

That afternoon Mike was waiting in a hallway at the county jail when a deputy brought George out of the lockup. "C'mon, George — they're letting you go!" Mike called out.

"Yeah? That's a relief! What happened?" George asked.

"I went to talk to Mr. Shelton. I told him what happened, and he and your dad talked to the sheriff and convinced him that you weren't involved in any of that stuff at the fairgrounds. Just a clueless bystander."

"Mr. Shelton did that for me?"

"Yeah. I think he secretly likes the fact that we're into music so much and that we have a band. Now let's go.

We've got to get your uncle's truck and get your piano loaded up. We'll need some gas money too. Should have filled up yesterday — it just went up to 29 cents a gallon!"

On an early evening in late May, with graduation drawing near, Ron and Ruby sat in the porch swing at her parents' home.

"Is anything wrong, Ron? You sounded awfully serious when you called."

Taking a folded sheet of paper from his shirt pocket, Ron said, "Well, it *is* kind of serious, Ruby. I needed to talk to you about it. This was waiting for me in the mail when I got home last night."

"What is it?"

Ron unfolded the letter and read out loud: "Greetings: You are hereby ordered for induction into the Armed Forces of the United States and to report at Fort Benning, Georgia." He slowly refolded the paper. "It's my draft notice."

"How can that be?" Ruby said, alarmed. "We don't even graduate until next week!"

"Well," he explained, "the thing is: I'm older than the rest of the kids in our class because I was held back a year in third grade. I had to register months ago when I turned 18."

She reached out and put her hand on his forearm. "But there are deferments and things — you don't *have* to go! You've always said you want to go to college and learn to be a great writer."

"I know," he said earnestly, "and it's probably crazy, but I don't want to be deferred; I want to go and do my part, just like my dad did in the big war." He paused. "Even though he got in toward the end and spent the whole time in Kansas."

Ruby was struggling to hold back tears. "But they'll send you to Vietnam — you know they will! You could get wounded, or even . . . ."

Ron pulled her close. "Come on, Ruby, you can't think about that. Last night on the news Cronkite said President Johnson wants to increase our troops over there from seventy-five thousand to a hundred and twenty-five thousand. With an army that big, by the time I get through basic training the war will probably be over!" He paused for a moment and then added, "You know, Hemingway said no fellow who thinks he wants to be a writer should miss the chance to go to war. That's what I think I want to do someday — write stories or maybe even novels. My dad thinks the army will be good for me, too. My mom's not very happy about it, though."

As Ruby began to regain her composure, Ron took both of her hands in his. "There's something else important I wanted to talk to you about, too. Since I have to leave soon." He took a deep breath. "I think we should get married before I go."

Surprised and uncertain, she whispered, "Oh, Ron."

"I know, I know," he said quickly. "We're really young and all that, but the very first time I saw you at that skating rink I knew there'd never be anyone else for me. I love you, Ruby, and I always will. And it would mean so much to me to know that you'll be here, as my wife — that I have someone I love to — to stand by me." He rose from the porch swing and then dropped to one knee.

"Ruby, I know we've only been together a short time, but I think when two people are right for each other, nothing else matters. Will you marry me?" He pulled a small jewelry box from the pocket of his chinos and held the ring out to her.

Smiling happily through her tears, Ruby said, "I do love you, Ron. And I always will." She paused. "Yes. Yes! I will marry you!"

As the 50th anniversary reunion drew to a close, the DJ played a recording of "The Party's Over," and classmates and their spouses began to say their goodbyes.

"You know, guys, this reunion has turned out to be a lot of fun — a nice little trip down memory lane," Dick commented.

"Yeah, I'd forgotten a lot of those things," Ron said.

"That fraternity dance at IU was the last big show for *The TrueTones*," Dick recalled.

George pulled Mike to one side and lowered his voice. "I know it's none of my business, but did you see Cathy anymore after you two broke up?"

"Well, I'd see her around school, but after graduation, no. Haven't seen her in all these years."

George glanced around conspiratorially. "You knew she got pregnant her senior year?"

Mike shook his head. "Really? No. No, I didn't know that. She always said it was a slippery slope."

"Yeah," George went on, "her and Tom Hoover. They didn't get married, though. You have to give her credit — she did everything on her own. Had the baby, got her diploma — even went to college. She's a nurse now." He motioned vaguely in the direction of downtown. "Works over at the Planned Parenthood."

They paused to shake hands with some of the other classmates who were passing by on their way to the exits. Then George continued, "And Tom Hoover became a NASCAR driver."

"No kidding!" Mike exclaimed. "Guess all that drag racing paid off, huh?"

"Well, not really," George said. "He died at a big race down in Alabama."

"Ooh, that's too bad," Mike said. "He crashed?"

"Nah," George shook his head. "Choked on a corndog."

More couples were saying their goodbyes and heading for the doors. Dick caught up with Ron and Ruby just before they reached the exit.

"Say, I'm sorry we didn't get to visit more," he said. "But looks like things worked out for you two. Ron obviously survived the war."

"Yep," Ron said, smiling. "Two grown kids and one grandchild. I worked my way up through the newspaper business. Always wanted to be a writer, but didn't know I would turn out to be a reporter or would wind up publishing my own newspaper some day. Ruby went into the real estate business and has done real well for herself. What about you?"

"Well, believe it or not, I went into teaching. Too much influence from Mr. Shelton, I guess. I'm band director now at the high school."

"No kidding! Well, that's great. Guess being in *The TrueTones* didn't ruin you musically."

"Listen," Dick went on, "I said something to the others — George and Mike, Patty and Renee, and some others — and we don't want to wait another five years for a reunion. We're going to plan something for next summer, maybe out at the lake. You think you would come?"

"Yeah, we'd like that," Ron said. "Count us in. Our group has something pretty special after going through all 12 years of school together. I think that creates a very special bond. Even though you may not even like a certain classmate sometimes, in the end you're all friends. Lifelong friends. We should definitely get together next summer."

They all started for the door as the janitor began turning off the lights around the perimeter of the gym.

"And Dick," Ron called out. "Be sure to bring your guitar!"

Big Break

For just a second, when he first opened his eyes, Lonnie didn't know where he was. Then, of course, he realized he had been sleeping on the couch in the living room of the one-bedroom mobile home he shared with his wife, Sally.

He started to sit up but was jolted by a sudden excruciating flash of pain in his left temple. Fortunately, it wasn't constant, seeming to strike only when he tried to move.

"Damn!" he thought, "feels like my brain is sloshing around inside my skull and crashing up against the side!"

He rose slowly, and gingerly walked down the short hallway to the trailer's cramped bathroom. He stood over the toilet, urinating, for an unusually long time. Suddenly he was overwhelmed by nausea. He dropped to his knees and vomited into the toilet bowl — mostly a gushing stream of last night's beer — then retched several more times until there was nothing left.

He stood and used his hand to direct water from the basin faucet to wash out his mouth.

As he walked out of the bathroom he was surprised to find his headache was gone. "Guess when I barfed it cleared all the poison out of my system," he thought.

His keys, cigarettes, some coins, and a butane lighter were lying on the end table by the couch. He lit his first Marlboro Light of the day and slipped the keys, lighter and change into the pocket of his faded jeans. He moved on to the kitchen and opened the fridge, which was nearly empty but did contain two bottles of beer. He opened one and went out the front door and sat on the metal steps, smoking and drinking.

He'd been there only a few minutes when a large, bright red box truck pulled up in front of the trailer, stopping partway in his yard, which was a mostly bare expanse of white sand scattered with cigarette butts and other debris and a few clumps of uncut grass and sandburs.

Large neon yellow lettering on the side of the truck proclaimed, "Wee Willie's Rent-to-Own: Furniture — Appliances — Electronics."

Two large young men got out of the truck and shuffled over to where Lonnie sat.

"Hey, Jeff! Hey, Bobby" Lonnie said as the two men approached.

Jeff was the older of the two, but not by much. Bobby was tall but pudgy with a round, innocent face that suggested he could have just graduated from high school.

"Hey, Lonnie — How ya doin'?" Jeff asked. Bobby hung back and didn't speak.

"I'm doin' alright," Lonnie said cautiously. "Want a beer?"

"No thanks. I don't usually drink beer in the morning," Jeff said. "We come about the couch."

"Aww, now, Jeff, you know I'm good for it," Lonnie protested. "I've got a show tomorrow night —Saturday night — at RJ's, and I'll be in with a payment first thing Monday morning."

"I wish we could do that," Jeff said, "but Willie laid down the law. He said if we didn't bring back the money this morning we damn sure better bring back the couch. You're way past due — three payments, not one. He ain't gonna take no more promises. But you'll have 30 days to make good on all the back payments and penalties if you want to reinstate the contract and get the couch back."

"But it's just until Monday, for Christ's sake!" Lonnie protested. "I'll have a couple hundred dollars at least by then." Lonnie stood up and tossed away his cigarette butt.

Bobby stood silently behind Jeff, obviously uncomfortable, staring intently at his shoes as the discussion continued.

"You know if it was up to me I'd go along with you," Jeff said, "but Willie ain't gonna take no for an answer, and that means we don't have any choice about it. We have to take the couch. It's nothing personal."

"Oh, it'll get personal when Sally gets home and finds out her couch is gone," Lonnie said. "She'll just kill me is all!"

"Now, I hope we can do this the easy way," Jeff said, waiting for a response from Lonnie. When no answer came, he added, "Or we can call the sheriff if we have to."

"No," Lonnie said, taking the last swig of beer. "You go ahead and do what you have to do."

Lonnie stood leaning his long skinny frame against the side of the mobile home, arms crossed, as the two men went inside and brought out the couch. He didn't stick around to watch them load it into the truck but went inside the trailer and slammed the door. A few minutes later he heard the truck drive away.

Lonnie brushed his teeth, shaved and showered, put on a clean western shirt with fake pearl snaps, and walked the seven blocks down to RJ's Dockside Bar and Grill. He entered through the back and found Dorothy, the day manager, preparing for the lunch crowd, filling individual ketchup bottles from a gallon plastic jug with a pump nozzle. Dorothy was an attractive woman in her forties who had learned the restaurant and bar business from the ground up and gained a no-nonsense attitude along the way. She had been at RJ's for almost 10 years and had no desire to work anywhere else. She was competent and comfortable in her job.

"Hey, Lonnie, how you doin'?" she asked as he let the screen door slam behind him.

"I'm great, Dorothy," he grinned. He went through the kitchen to look into the bar and dining area. "I see a few regulars starting to drift in," he commented.

Then he turned back to Dorothy. "RJ been in yet?"

"No," she said. "He probably won't come in till about three, see how we did for lunch, and then stick around for the night shift."

"I just wanted to be sure we were clear about my music gig for tomorrow night," Lonnie explained.

"Oh, yes — that's right!" Dorothy responded. "It's already on the marquee out front. That reminds me — have you seen Shirley?"

Shirley was one of the night waitresses.

"No, not for a couple of days," Lonnie said.

Dorothy's expression was animated. "Well, she's all excited about this guy who's in town visiting her brother. This fellow's from Nashville, Tennessee, and Shirley told him about you, and he wants to come and hear you sing."

"Really?" Lonnie asked. "What kind of guy is he?"

"Well, I don't know much," Dorothy said. "Just that he's from Nashville and has some connection to the music business. I haven't met him yet. You should give Shirley a call. Who knows? She thinks this might be your big break!"

Her enthusiasm made Lonnie smile.

"Yeah, I'll call her, see what the deal is. There's a lot of these music business guys who talk big, but it's all bullshit. You have to be careful. I'll give her a call, though. You never know; he could be legit."

Walking home, Lonnie daydreamed about what it could mean to have a solid connection in Nashville — a chance to get out of Tybee and Savannah, to get his songs heard — and recorded and promoted and played on the radio; touring all over the country, having money and the nice things money could buy for him and Sally. "Doesn't hurt to dream," he thought.

For the last block and a half as he approached the mobile home he could see Sally sitting on the front steps, and he felt pretty sure her expression was growing steadily angrier as he approached. When he reached the edge of the yard, she exclaimed, "You let them take our couch?"

She stood and leaned slightly toward him, her face red with fury. "You let those morons just come in here and take the couch right out of our living room?"

Lonnie raised his hands in front of his chest as if surrendering. "Hey, I tried to stop them. I told them I had a gig this weekend, and I'd be able to pay, but they said they couldn't wait — orders from Willie. There wasn't anything I could do."

Sally paced in a circle, her blue canvas shoes plopping in the sand. "Well, I'm sure you got that right — there was nothing you could do. There's never anything you can do!"

"Aww, Sally. I'll go down there Monday and work something out. If I offer them cash they're not going to turn it down. I'll get your couch back."

She stopped pacing. "Sure, you'll get it back — if you pay more than it's worth in rent and late fees. They'll probably even charge you for bringing it back! If we ever do get that thing paid off, it will be the most expensive couch anyone ever bought, and by then it'll be falling apart!"

She stomped into the trailer and slammed the door behind her, but after a couple of minutes she came back out with the last cold beer in her hand, shut the door, and sat on the steps. "We have to talk about this right now," she said angrily. She took a sip of the beer.

"I told you: I'll fix it Monday," Lonnie said softly.

"I'm not talking about the couch," she snapped. "I'm talking about the fact that you aren't making any money — you don't even bring home enough to make payments on a stupid-ass rent-to-own sofa!"

"I'll have some money after Saturday night," Lonnie said defensively.

"What? Playing one night at RJ's?" She pointed the beer bottle at him as if threatening him with it. "What about after that?"

He started to speak, but she cut him off.

"There's *nothing* after that. That's the problem!" she spat. "He won't hire you more than once a week because he either can't afford a band every night or doesn't want the same one every time. We can't live on two hundred dollars a week, and even that's hit and miss!"

"I can get other gigs," Lonnie argued.

"Well, that hasn't worked out, has it?" Sally shot

back. "There aren't that many options here, you know. And some of them don't want country — they want pop or jazz or rock or whatever. It's not like they don't know you're available — every bar owner in Tybee and Savannah knows who you are — but they're not calling, are they?"

"It doesn't work that way," Lonnie said. "I need to do a better job of keeping after them."

"No," Sally said, standing again and giving him a fierce look. "You need to do a better job of getting a real job — something where you get paid every week, enough to pay our bills, and not just every now and then. You know I don't make enough at the flower shop to cover everything."

"Sally, listen —"

"No, Lonnie, you listen to me!" she insisted. "Bill Thorne has a job for you at Chu's hardware store. All you have to do is go down there and start helping him with the inventory. If you don't screw that up, he'll put you to work full time. It's not a huge salary, but it's decent pay, and it'll be something we can count on. With that and what I make at the shop we'll be able to pay our bills and have some kind of normal life, like normal people, without worrying that someone's going to come and take our couch!"

Lonnie stood silently, staring at his boots.

"He has to do this inventory at night, when the store's closed," Sally explained. "You'll work 5 p.m. until 1 a.m. tonight and Saturday, and all day Sunday, and that'll take care of the inventory. Then you start the regular day shift on Monday, just generally helping out in the store."

"I dunno, Sally —"

"You'll work a regular eight to five shift once you get started, and you can still play music on nights and weekends if you want," she added.

She stood on the steps, reached for the doorknob, and then turned back to Lonnie. "I need you to understand, Lonnie, that this is serious. I love you, and I've tried to stand by you, but if you let me down this time, I'm leaving. I mean it. If you don't take that job this weekend and stick with it, I'll be on a bus back to Macon. I'll stay with Mom and Dad for a while and get a job there. I'm not kidding. I'm not going to live like this anymore."

She stormed back inside and slammed the door behind her.

Lonnie sat on the front steps for a while, smoking a cigarette and searching his mind for some sort of workable solution that didn't involve the hardware store. Finally, he got up, crossed the street and walked down to a public bench overlooking the marsh. He sat, flipped open his phone and called Shirley, the waitress.

"Hi, Shirl," he said when she answered. "It's Lonnie. Dorothy said you had some news about some guy from Nashville."

"Yeah, he's up here visiting, and my sister Penny told him about you. He seemed interested and said he'd like to meet you, maybe come hear you play."

"What's he do in Nashville?"

"Well, I don't know that he's in the music business himself, but his family is. He might be able to put you in touch with some people who could really help you."

"Well, I'd like to check him out too, try to see if he's legit, you know?"

"That's fine," Shirley said. "He asked me if we could all have lunch tomorrow at Fannie's. And then if he thinks it's worth pursuing, he'll come to hear you tomorrow night."

"Yeah, I guess that'd be alright. What time, noon?"

"He said eleven-thirty would be good."

"Okay. See you then. Thanks."

When Lonnie got back to the trailer he found Sally at the kitchen sink, washing a few dishes. She called to him over her shoulder, "Don't forget, you've got to be at the hardware store at five so Bill can show you the ropes. Don't be late."

Shortly before five Lonnie trudged down to the store, where the manager welcomed him with a friendly smile and handshake.

"We have to do this inventory for tax reasons," Thorne explained, "which basically means we have to count everything in the store." He motioned around to the many aisles of shelves filled with thousands of items. "You can't do it with customers coming and going, so we have to do it at night, after closing. But you help me get through this next couple of days, and we might have something for you on the regular daytime shift."

He handed Lonnie a clipboard, escorted him to one of the aisles, and showed him how to tally the products on the inventory form.

"You have to take time to be accurate," Thorne explained, "but you can't dilly-dally either. You'll get the rhythm of it after a while — fast but accurate."

When Lonnie left the store at 1 a.m. he felt as if swarms of numbers were swirling behind his eyes. Once inside the trailer, he took off his boots and lay down next to Sally. Within minutes he was sound asleep.

When he awoke, Sally had already left for work, and Lonnie had only an hour to get ready for his lunch meeting.

When he walked through the door at Fannie's on the Beach, he immediately spotted Shirley and the stranger in a booth near the front window. They were both sitting on the same side of the table. The Nashville man, probably in his fifties, had salt-and-pepper hair and a ruddy face that suggested a fondness for whiskey. As Lonnie approached the table, the man half rose, clutching his napkin with his left hand and extending his right. "Lonnie?" he said. "I'm Lyndell Stearns. Nice to meet you."

Lonnie shook the man's hand. "Good to meet you, too. Hi, Shirley, how you doin'?"

Shirley just smiled and nodded, and Lonnie took the seat opposite the two of them.

"Shirley and her sister been tellin' me you've got a lot of talent when it comes to country music," Stearns said. "They think you might be interested in trying your luck in Nashville."

"Well, sure," Lonnie said. "Who wouldn't want to get their music heard there if they could."

"What kind of music do you play?"

"I mostly play in the bars in Savannah and here in Tybee, so I have to do mostly covers — classic country. People want to hear songs they're familiar with, but I slip in an original tune here and there, and some of them have picked up a pretty good following. It's always good when someone asks for one of my original songs."

Stearns beamed. "That's great that you write some of your own tunes. That means you get to keep more of the royalties. Always a good thing."

A waiter approached the booth, and Stearns said, "Order whatever you want. Lunch is on me."

"Shrimp burger and fries," Lonnie told the waiter without looking at a menu. "And a Coastal Empire ale."

As the young man walked away, Lonnie asked Stearns, "What is it that you do in Nashville? Shirley wasn't sure."

"Well it's actually my brother-in-law. You may have heard of him — Sonny Jackson?" When Lonnie didn't react, Stearns went on. "He used to play steel guitar in Willy Nelson's band. Toured with Willy for nearly ten years. Now he has his own recording studio and record label."

"That sounds good."

"Oh yeah, if he likes your music he can get you out of Tybee, record your songs, and you'll be touring all over the country. Bigger, nicer venues, too — none of these hole-in-the-wall bars."

Stearns leaned forward, his elbows on the table. "Sonny takes good care of his artists. He's even got a gal who'll pick out wardrobe for you, give you that authentic Nashville 'look.' By the way, what kind of guitar do you play?"

"A Taylor," Lonnie said. "It's a pretty nice guitar."

Stearns shook his head. "Sonny'll probably get you an endorsement deal, maybe with Gibson or — who knows? — Collings even."

"Martin?" Lonnie asked.

"Nah," Stearns scoffed. "Everybody's got a Martin these days. You want something different that stands out — a Larrivee, maybe. "I don't know, we'll see."

"That all sounds great," Lonnie said, grinning.

"You know if everything works out, and you get a recording deal and go out on tour, that's a whole different life than just playing in bars on weekends." Stearns leaned back and linked his fingers across his belly. "It can be hard on relationships because you're gone all the time. It can be just plain exhausting, too. You'll play in some town one night and then immediately drive 300 miles to do another show the next night. It can be a grind. You think you're up for all that?"

Lonnie leaned forward, his expression serious. "Music is my life, man," he said. "It's everything for me. When I'm out there on stage, and my band is in the groove, and you can feel the audience sailing right along with you — there's nothing else like it. Not liquor, not pot, not religion — nothing. Not even sex. It's like you're one with the universe, Mr. Stearns, or one with God, even. It's what I live for."

"Okay," Stearns said, smiling. "You sound ready to me. So, what time's your show tonight?"

"I go on at nine."

"Well, I'll be there. If you're as good as Shirley here says you are, I'll get you in touch with Sonny, and we'll go from there. Sky's the limit, as they say!"

From Fannie's, Lonnie headed down the street toward the pier, intending to cut through an alley to get back to his trailer. As he passed by the big wooden stairs going up onto the pier, powerful hands grabbed his arms and dragged him behind the staircase.

"Hey, boys!" Lonnie cried out. "What's going on?"

He was being held against the rough timber underpinnings of the pier by two large black men in jeans and Hawaiian shirts.

"Leon ain't happy with you," one of the men growled. "Says you been avoidin' him."

"By that he means you ain't paid back what you borrowed," the other man added. "Leon says 'time's up'."

"Maurice and me had to drive out here from Savannah to hunt you down," the first man said. "Lucky for us, you ain't hard to find."

"Hey, Maurice," Lonnie pleaded, "you and Darnell know I'm good for what I owe. And Leon knows it too. There's no need for rough stuff!"

"Yeah, but it's gettin' there," Maurice answered. "You're almost to the point it's gonna start doubling every week. And we all know you can't keep up with that."

"So you got to do somethin' now," Darnell added.

"Guys, I'm gonna have money coming in. You gotta believe me. I just need a little more time. I'm looking at a record deal that'll get me fair and square with everybody!"

"A record deal!" Darnell scoffed. "What you gonna do? Sell all your old LP's?"

"No, I'm serious, man! There's a guy from Nashville in town right now, and he's coming to my show tonight at RJ's."

"Seriously?" Maurice said. He shook his head. "I don't know if we can sell that idea to Leon. He wants his money, not some half-assed scheme."

"How much you gettin' for playing tonight?" Darnell asked. "Couple hundred?"

"Yeah."

"Well, it ain't much, but it's better than nothin'." He released Lonnie's arm. "Maurice and me wouldn't get no pleasure out'a bustin' you up, kid, but you need to understand it's headed that way, and pretty damn fast, okay? Leon's not a patient man."

Maurice released Lonnie's other arm. "We'll be

countin' on that two hundred, so don't even think about tryin' to skip out on us," he warned.

"Hey, I'm just tryin' to do business with you the best I can, fellows," Lonnie said.

The two big men nodded and started walking away, and Lonnie breathed a huge sigh of relief.

As the five o'clock hour approached, Lonnie headed reluctantly toward the hardware store, knowing a confrontation with Thorne was inevitable. He began his shift as usual, picking up his clipboard and working his way along an aisle displaying all shapes, sizes and types of plumbing fixtures. All the while he kept an eye on the big black and white wall clock as the hours ticked by. At eight-thirty he went to find Thorne.

He held out the clipboard. "Bill, I'm sorry, but I've got to leave early tonight," he said.

"What?"

"There's something I have to do. I can't get out of it. But I'll come back after. I already finished aisle seven."

Thorne was frowning, and his jaw was clenched in anger. "How long is this 'thing' going to take?"

"I'll be done around midnight."

"And your shift's over at one, so there's no point coming back." He snatched the clipboard from Lonnie's hand. "You know I only offered to try this for Sally's sake, and you can't even stick with it for two full days! Jesus Christ!"

Shaking his head, Thorne started to walk away but

then turned back. "I can't deal with someone as unreliable as you. If you leave here now, don't bother ever coming back. I don't ever want to see you in this store again." He stormed off toward his office.

Lonnie let himself out and walked away into the night.

Sally answered her phone to hear an angry Bill Thorne saying, "I'm sorry to have to tell you this, Sally, but . . . "

When their conversation ended, she went to the closet and pulled out a battered suitcase. There were tears in her eyes as she angrily packed her things, but the set of her jaw was determined.

When Lonnie arrived at the bar, the band members were on stage setting up. Lonnie surveyed the room through a peephole in the curtain at the back of the stage.

He immediately spotted the man from Nashville and Shirley at a table in front of the stage. Stearns looked as if he had already had a few drinks. His right arm was draped loosely over Shirley's shoulders, and he was mumbling something in her ear. She looked uncomfortable and pushed his hand away from time to time when it slipped from her shoulder toward her breast.

There were couples at three other tables, but the rest were unoccupied. Several men were huddled over drinks at the bar, looking up occasionally at a television screen that showed a football game with no sound.

Silently, the Brevard brothers — Maurice and Darnell — entered the main door at the back of the barroom and took a table near the rear wall. The big men sat without speaking, their hands folded on the table in front of them, eyes scanning the room.

The man from Nashville continued to fumble, trying to pull Shirley closer to him, his head bobbing drunkenly.

Lonnie heard his drummer, Billy Skaggs, clicking his sticks together to set the tempo as the band launched into the rollicking introduction to "All My Rowdy Friends Are Comin' Over Tonight," the music they always used to usher Lonnie onstage.

Lonnie could feel the bass notes throbbing in his chest. The drumbeat was crisp and clean, and the lead guitar was kicking up the excitement.

Billy pulled his mic close and yelled, "Ladies and gentlemen! RJ's Dockside Bar and Grill — Tybee's premier music venue — is proud to present Nashville's next big country star: Lonnie Donovan!"

As the music continued to wail and pulsate, Lonnie bounded onto the stage. He snatched his vocal mic from its stand and, looking out over the room, cried, "Good evening, everybody! Thanks for coming out! I'm really happy to be here!"

O, Holy Night

"Miss Harper! Miss Harper!"

She turned and saw the principal, Mr. Hardebeck, scurrying toward her, zig-zagging through groups of students who were return-ing to class after a rehearsal of the annual Christmas program.

Mr. Hardebeck was a small, tidy man with sparse, slicked-back, graying hair. He wore thin, wire-rimmed spectacles and a navy pinstriped suit, and his small feet were tightly bound in shiny black dress shoes which clicked out a rapid rhythm on the hardwood floor of the old elementary school as he approached.

He glanced around and then strode quickly to the door of her nearby classroom and waited for her to en-ter. Because her students had art instruction in the cafeteria this period, the room was empty.

"Miss Harper," he began as he turned and closed the door, "I know this is your first year here, but I must tell you that several of the other teachers are very upset about your plans for the Christmas program."

"Why, I wasn't aware of any problems," she responded. "We've barely started rehearsals."

He leaned toward her conspiratorially. "I've been told you plan to use the Paxton boy in one of the tableaux," he asserted, "on stage."

"Well, yes — possibly as one of the shepherds," she admitted hesitantly, still uncertain where the conversation was going.

"Well, we just don't think that's a good idea," he huffed.

Miss Harper felt her initial apprehension turning now to fear and anger. "And why is it not a good idea?" she asked.

He pursed his lips. "As I said, I know you've been here only a short time, but you must have noticed that the boy is not normal. He's mentally backward, he moves awkwardly, he often behaves inappropriately, and he can become loud and disruptive. It's just not wise to place him in a highly visible role in an important program like this. And besides, we've always given the on-stage roles to the better students in each class as a sort of reward or recognition."

"I've had Benny in class," she said slowly. "He may not be as bright as some of the other children, but I've found him to be very interested in everything we're doing in the classroom and very eager to please. I'm sure being in this pageant would mean a great deal to him."

"You must realize, Miss Harper, that the Christmas program is our most important event of the year," Principal Hardebeck persisted. "The entire community turns out for this. The county superintendent will be here, all the school board members and their wives, all the downtown business people, the councilmen, all the parents — everyone."

Mr. Hardebeck drew himself up to his full height and continued, "This year's program may be especially important to the community, with the country in the grip of this horrible Depression — so many out of work, farmers struggling to survive, businesses going under. This may be our best opportunity to provide something uplifting, some escape from the bleak world outside."

She struggled to blink back tears and keep her voice from shaking. "So you are telling me I absolutely may not have Benny play one of the shepherds?"

"Miss Harper, I understand that you are very young and have not had much experience with the public, but the fact is that this boy makes people uncomfortable. We can't let one person spoil the program for everyone."

She stared down at her hands. "If I have to tell him he can't be a shepherd it will break his heart," she said.

"Not at all," Mr. Hardebeck beamed. "I'm sure he will be just as happy sitting in the bleachers with all the other boys and girls. You can find a way to smooth it over with him."

He waited for her to respond, but she remained silent. Finally, he turned, opened the door, and then turned back to her. "So. We're agreed then?" he asked.

"No, sir," she said quietly. "We are not agreed at all, but I suppose if I am to be employed here I must do as I'm told."

He stared coldly at her for a moment. "Very well then." He left the room and closed the door behind him.

Miss Harper spent the night in torment, going over her conversation with Mr. Hardebeck, trying to think how she might have responded differently, how she could have stood up to him, made him understand. And she agonized, also without success, about what she would tell Benny, how she could break it to him painlessly. And she was not prepared the next day when he burst into her classroom unexpectedly before the morning bell had rung.

"Miss Harper!"

She was writing a list of spelling words on the blackboard when she turned and saw him in the doorway. Benny was small for his age. He had an unruly shock of red hair and pale, freckled skin. When he walked his shoulders tilted to one side, and he held his head at an awkward angle. His left foot turned outward and dragged slightly behind him. His voice was high, shrill, and breathy with a nasal, almost bleating quality. Miss Harper once had to scold a group of students who had surrounded Benny on the playground and were having cruel fun mimicking his mannerisms and way of speaking. But this morning his smile was radiant.

"Miss Harper! Are we going to have Christmas practice today?"

Her heart ached, and her face burned with shame for taking part in what she felt was a petty conspiracy.

"Yes, Benny," she said. "We'll have a rehearsal again this afternoon." She looked into his face and tried to sound enthusiastic. "But there's been a change of plans." Her mind was spinning furiously as she tried to find an explanation less hurtful than the truth.

"Some of the teachers," she began, "are concerned about the fourth grade chorus. They have to sing "O, Holy Night" at the end of the program, and it's a very important moment, and — well, some of the teachers think we don't have enough good singers, and they wanted me to ask you if you would help. I mean, anyone can stand up there on stage like a statue, but they need someone to help sing."

She looked at him imploringly, afraid that he would see through her feeble proposal and be devastated, but to her amazement his smile grew even brighter.

"I can sing!" he blurted confidently. "I can sing, Miss Harper! I can sing 'O, Holy Night'!"

"Oh, good, Benny. That's such a relief! I'm so glad you don't mind switching parts. I know you'll be a big help to the chorus." She was so relieved that the difficult moment had passed that she was now anxious for him to leave so she could compose herself.

"I want to sing 'O, Holy Night!" Benny persisted.

She patted his shoulder. "And you will, Benny. You and all the fourth graders will sing it, and I know you'll all do very well."

"No, Miss Harper! I want to sing 'O, Holy Night.' Just me! I want to sing it all by myself! I already know how it goes. I can sing good!"

Her heart sank. "Oh, Benny. I don't know. I don't think that would be a good idea. To sing a solo in front of all those people? Oh, no. I don't think I could even do that — I would be too nervous. It will be much better if you just sing with all the others."

But he was adamant.

"I want to sing 'O, Holy Night'! All by myself! Just me!"

She didn't know what to do. She had not heard Benny sing, but she could imagine how his voice would sound.

"That's just not possible, Benny!" she said, forcing herself to be more firm. "You just have to settle for being a part of the chorus. I'm sorry, but that's the way it has to be!"

She could see the disappointment burning in his eyes. He mumbled, "I can sing," then turned and ran from the room.

"This is almost worse than it was before," Miss Harper thought. She sat at her desk, put her face in her hands, and wept.

Every day for the next three weeks the children

practiced their parts in the Christmas program. When the fourth graders sang, Benny sat silent, staring at the floor, his face blank.

Soon the big night arrived. Throughout the day, excitement crackled through the classrooms and hall-ways of the school. As people began arriving that night, snow began to fall, adding an even more magical atmo-sphere to the festivities.

Some families arrived in old cars or pickup trucks, some in horse-drawn buggies or farm wagons. The school bus even ran its route that night, picking up entire families. How strange it seemed to the children to see grownups — parents — riding the bus to school. A steady stream of children and adults passed under the street light in front of the old building and quickly filled the small gymnasium where the Christmas pro-gram would be held.

Miss Harper stood in her classroom, looking out the window, down the wide sidewalk to the street, watching the snow swirling in the glow of the streetlights as the families arrived. She saw work-hardened men feeling a little sheepish in their Sunday best, their faces scrubbed and their hair carefully combed. Others wore what they had — work boots, bib overalls, and heavy denim work coats. A few — the businessmen from town — wore suits and ties, overcoats and fedoras.

And then she saw the Paxtons — Benny and his mother and father, an older brother, a little sister — as they approached the school on foot, talking and laughing, with Benny in the center, hitching himself along in his unique bobbing and weaving gait.

Although she smiled, at the same time she felt a sense of sadness and loss. She had counted herself fortunate to find a teaching job here at a time when there were few jobs to be had. She had hoped to build a career in this school and in this community, to become a part of its life. But now she was troubled by a nagging sense of having failed in that role by going along with a decision she knew was wrong and unfair.

As she turned away from the window, her fiancé appeared in the classroom door. "Everything looks really beautiful!" he said, smiling broadly.

He crossed to her and took one of her hands in both of his. "I guess you got everything worked out for the program?"

"Supposedly," she said. "But I still don't feel right about it, David. Having a bigger part would have meant so much to Benny. People just can't see what a great kid he is. And now that he isn't allowed to be on stage, I also had to tell him he can't sing a solo like he wanted. He was so disappointed."

"Well," David said, frowning, "he *is* different. And you can't go against Mr. Hardebeck. You need this job. *We* need this job. You don't want to do anything to mess up our future."

He gave her a quick hug and turned to leave. "Don't

worry," he said. "It'll all be over in an hour or so, and we can put this behind us. You'll see."

In the gym, the smell of damp woolen coats and gloves filled the air as spectators filed into bleachers on either side and folding chairs on the center floor, all facing the stage at the south end of the gym where various scenes from the Christmas story would be portrayed. Several sections of bleachers were reserved for the elementary school classes. Only a handful of students would appear on stage as narrators, angels, Mary and Joseph, wise men, or shepherds; the rest would remain in the side bleachers with their classmates. Each class — first through sixth grades — would sing one or two songs at designated times during the pageant.

The program opened with the narrator telling how an angel appeared to Mary and told her that she would bear a son and that she should call his name Jesus. A girl with beautiful blond curls proudly wore the gleaming white angel costume with glittery wings standing over a prayerful Mary as the narrator recounted the familiar story.

In the next scene, Joseph and Mary were shown on their way to Bethlehem. The shop class at the high school had made a painted plywood cutout in the shape of a donkey. A wooden stool was placed behind the cutout so that Mary could appear to be sitting on the donkey. While the actors remained motionless on stage, the first graders sang "Oh, Little Town of Bethlehem."

Subsequent scenes portrayed the arrival of Mary and Joseph at the inn, the birth of the baby Jesus, the announcement to the shepherds, and the arrival of the wise men, accompanied by two plywood camels. Music by the various classes included "It Came Upon a Midnight Clear," "We Three Kings," and "Joy to the World."

Just before the pageant began, pupils in Miss Harper's class were lined up in the hallway just outside the doors to the gym. As she started to open the doors so the students could file in, she suddenly shook her head, looked upward briefly, and turned back to face the children.

"Class!" she said in a loud stage whisper. "Listen, children! There's been a change in plans. When it's time for 'O, Holy Night,' we're going to let Benny sing it, okay? Everyone understand? Benny, are you sure you can do this?"

Benny, halfway back in the line of children, nodded enthusiastically. The other children looked skeptical and whispered among themselves, shaking their heads.

"Alright then," Miss Harper said firmly. She took a deep breath and added, "Let's go." The children filed into the gym and took their seats in the bleachers.

As time for the final song grew near, Miss Harper stood in the wings, her hands clasped beneath her chin, nervously twisting a small lace handkerchief.

Then the pianist turned and nodded to the fourth grade class. She adjusted a page of sheet music and began the introduction to "O, Holy Night."

The children began to sing, but after a moment — one by one — their voices fell still as they became aware of a miraculous sound coming from their midst.

O, Holy night, the stars are brightly shining;
It is the night of our dear Savior's birth.

A hush fell over the auditorium as the high, pure sound of a single child's voice rose and fell, soaring into the gym's steel rafters and swooping among the spectators who sat agape, captivated by the angelic melody.

Long lay the world in sin and error pining,
'Till He appeared and the soul felt its worth.

Heads turned as the audience strained to locate the source of the incredible voice. Members of the fourth grade class stood silently, staring in awe at their classmate as Benny sang:

A thrill of hope, the weary world rejoices
For yonder breaks a new and glorious morn.

As the song began, Mr. Hardebeck had risen from his seat in surprise, frowning, but now he stood transfixed by a voice he could not fathom. Standing in the shadows at the edge of the stage, Miss Harper also looked about in confusion until her eyes settled on Benny's rapturous face. "It's a miracle!" she whispered. But then she wondered, "Or have you always had this gift and we were all just too busy to notice?"

Fall on your knees, O hear the angel voices.

Women in the audience wept openly while the men swallowed hard and clenched their jaws, caught off guard by the intense emotion surrounding them. One old farmer with a leathery, weathered face and two-day stubble of gray whiskers wiped his eyes with a crumpled red bandanna. A local merchant felt himself transported back to his native land, where he had heard such voices before in a great cathedral.

And the music continued, climbing to a spectacular finale as the child sang:

O, night divine; O-oh night when Christ was born,
O night, divine, Oh-Oh-Oh night . . .O night
divine . . .

The final notes faded away into total silence. The pianist sat staring at her keyboard, tears streaming down her face. On the other side of the gym a little boy reached up and took his mother's hand. A very old man standing in the doorway under the exit sign slowly nodded his head in affirmation. Benny stood in the center of the front row of the fourth grade, smiling brightly, still intrigued by the nativity scene that had remained frozen on stage.

The silence finally ended when a man in the far upper corner of the bleachers began to clap very slowly, and others gradually joined in, until the entire crowd was standing and applauding wildly — including Benny and the other children, the teachers, the actors on stage, and even Mr. Hardebeck.

During Christmas break the Paxtons moved to Salem, where Mr. Paxton had found work cutting logs for one of President Roosevelt's public works projects, and we never heard Benny sing again. Miss Harper continued to teach at our school for nearly 40 years and, although Mr. Hardebeck never mentioned what happened at the pageant, parents and former students often recalled with her their fond memories of that special night when Benny sang his song.

Darkroom

"Hey, Murph!"

John Murphy turned away from his typewriter to find managing editor Charlie Davers invading his tiny cubicle.

"I've got a surprise for you!" Davers continued, smiling broadly. He placed a package on Murphy's desk. Murphy didn't say anything, he just looked up, curious.

"We're gonna start loading our own rolls of 35 millimeter film," Davers announced. "They said it will save us a lot of money compared to buying packaged film." He removed the top of the cardboard box in which the items had been shipped.

"See? This is a hundred-foot roll of Tri-X film, and it comes with these reloadable 35 millimeter canisters and a loader with a hand crank. You can load twenty-four, thirty-six — even just ten or twelve frames if that's all you're going to need for an assignment. Eliminate a lot of waste."

"Sounds like extra work," Murphy said.

"Not really. Once you get used to it, it'll be routine. I've got a meeting now, but we'll try it out this afternoon so you can see how it works, okay? It's gonna be great; you'll see!"

Murphy returned to his typing, putting the finishing touches on his account of that morning's county commissioners' meeting. Such reports were a mainstay of the small town newspaper, and Murphy spent much of his time covering local units of government — town council, school board, county commissioners. He liked to say that he had attended more school board meetings than most board members.

There wasn't a lot of "hard news" in Riverton — the occasional serious traffic accident, house fire, or court trial and, perhaps every fifteen or twenty years, a murder.

Murphy took the pages of his completed commissioners' story to the composing room and handed them to Reva, the typesetter.

"Here you go, Reva," he said. "If Charlie comes looking for me, tell him I've gone to lunch."

It was a warm, early October day, and the huge old maple trees in the courthouse yard were decked out in blazing red and orange. With each breeze, a few leaves fluttered down, settling softly on the grass. The longtime mom and pop restaurant on the far side of the courthouse square was busy with lunchtime traffic, waitresses carrying trays loaded with food, scurrying from the kitchen to waiting customers at tables and booths. The sounds of clinking tableware and multiple simultaneous conversations filled the room, along with the savory smell of fried foods.

Murphy sat on a stool at the counter to order his burger and fries. When he had finished his lunch and was standing at the register paying his tab, he saw a short, white-haired man leaving the restaurant.

On the sidewalk outside, Murphy called: "Hey, Doc!"

Dr. Frank Ellis, one of two general practitioners in town, stopped and turned.

"Oh, hi, John," he said.

"I don't mean to hold you up," Murphy said. "Just have a quick question."

The doctor raised his bushy white eyebrows inquisitively.

"Yeah," Murphy continued, "I didn't want to take up your time with an office visit since all I wanted was to ask if you would refill my diet pill prescription."

The eyebrows rose again.

"Doesn't look to me like you need any more diet pills," Ellis said. "Can't say precisely, of course, but your weight at this point appears to be in good proportion to your height."

"Well, I'm not quite there yet. If I could just get another thirty days . . ."

"That concerns me, John. These amphetamines are not something to take lightly. We're finding out they're very habit-forming, and they can lead to some serious complications."

Murphy tugged nervously at his collar.

"That's why I was thinking, Doc, if I could just have another thirty days I could give them up gradually and not all at once. Maybe that would be the best way."

"This isn't something we can discuss adequately out here in the street," the doctor said. "Make an appointment, and we'll sit down and consider all the options. Okay?"

Dr. Ellis turned and walked away toward his office, and Murphy stood watching him go, clenching and unclenching his hands.

Editor Davers was waiting when Murphy made it back to the newspaper office.

They both went into the darkroom, and Davers explained how to place the big roll of black-and-white film into the loader — a part of the process that had to be done in complete darkness.

"After that you can turn the light back on," Davers said.

"Then you open this little light-safe door on top, and an empty film cartridge can be clicked into place and filled by simply turning the crank on the side of the loader."

He demonstrated how this was done, and handed the newly filled cartridge to Murphy.

"The most important thing to remember," Davers emphasized, "is that, if you let any light get to the film at any point, it'll be ruined, but you won't know that until you develop it. And then it's too late. Whatever pictures you took will be ruined. So you need to be methodical and take it step by step."

Murphy spent the rest of the afternoon typing obits and rewriting press releases that had come in the mail or by fax. He gave the pages to Reva and left a little early since he had to photograph a football game that night. The paper's part-time sports editor, Jerry "Sox" Baker, would write up the game. Murphy just had to contribute a couple of decent action shots.

His apartment was on the third floor of one of the brick business buildings that lined Main Street facing the front of the courthouse. It consisted of a kitchen-dining-living room area, a small bathroom, and one very small bedroom.

He got a beer from the fridge, sat at the dining table, and popped the cap off a pill bottle. He spilled the brightly colored pills into his hand. Only three left. He took one, washing it down with beer.

The pills usually made him feel energized, but for several nights he'd been having trouble sleeping, and his legs were tired and achy. He went into the other room and stretched out on the bed, thinking he could get a little rest before the ballgame. Maybe it would get rid of his headache, too.

When it was time to head over to the high school, he decided to walk. The weather was pleasant, and it wasn't that far. He cut across town diagonally, through residential neighborhoods — some older, some relatively new. He was passing by one older two-story house when he heard voices, apparently coming from inside. He shouldn't have been able to hear them, he thought. He never had before. It was as if he suddenly had some sort of super hearing.

"Supper's ready, Larry! Go wash your hands," a woman's voice called. "Tell your sister to come down."

As he passed the next house he heard, "John, did you check the mailbox when you came in?"

"Yeah, I did. Nothing but bills, as always."

"Now John, don't be grumpy."

From the next house he heard a man saying, almost in a whisper, "You know I love you, Marie."

And Marie answered, softly, "I know you do, Phil. I'm just not sure I'm ready for this." Murphy could actually hear their kisses, and then even more passionate sounds.

As he walked on, Murphy thought, "This is really odd. They must all have their windows wide open, not caring who hears their conversations. And it's all so boring, so mundane!"

In the next block he passed by a newer one-story brick ranch. He heard a girl's voice saying, "Daddy, did you see that man?"

"Huh? What man?" Apparently that was the father's voice.

"There's a man in front of our house. And he has a camera! Should we call the police?"

Murphy walked faster, leaving that block behind, and soon reached the high school parking lot. All along the way he glanced around nervously, expecting to see an approaching police car.

But as usual at games, the town marshal's car was parked along the curb near the pedestrian entrance to the football stadium. The marshal was leaning against the rear fender, watching the stream of fans entering the gate. He turned as Murphy approached. "Hi, Murph," he said. "Working the game?"

"Yeah, get a few pictures," Murphy muttered. Lowering his head, he hurried through the gate, signed in, and took his place on the sideline near the home team's bench.

After the game, Murphy filed out of the stadium with the rest of the crowd. As he reached the end of the long sidewalk where the parking lot met the street, he saw a man standing under a streetlamp, smoking a cigarette.

He knew who it was: Bud Robison. They had been in high school at the same time, although not in the same class. Bud was one of the rough kids from the lower end of town, down by the paper mill. In recent years, Murphy had seen Robison's name in the arrest reports published in the paper — public intoxication, disorderly conduct, battery. And drug offenses.

Murphy approached him tentatively. Robison turned and gave him a hard look, frowning. "Murphy?" he asked as recognition sank in. "What the hell do you want?"

"Hey, Bud, I just saw you here, and I thought you might be able to help me with some information."

"You still work for *The Journal?*" When Murphy nodded yes, Robison said, "I don't know anything you'd be interested in, and if I did I wouldn't tell you."

"This has nothing to do with the paper," Murphy insisted. "It's just information I need, personally."

"That's just weird, man, what are you talking about?"

"No offense, Bud, but I was hoping you could tell me where I could get more of my diet pills."

"Diet pills? Are you shittin' me?"

"Well, technically I guess they're called amphetamines. That's what Doc Ellis calls them. I started taking them to lose weight, but now I'm running out, and he won't give me any more."

"So you want to go out on the street and buy some speed, and since I'm the big druggie around town you thought I'd be able to get you some. Is that it?"

"No, no, no," Murphy insisted. "It's not like that. I didn't even think of it till I saw you standing here. I just thought you might know stuff like that — kind of through the grapevine."

"You'd be breaking the law, you know. And I'd be breaking the law if I helped you."

"No one would know. No one would ever find out," Murphy argued.

"I don't know," Robison said, shaking his head.

"Being a reporter you're pretty tight with the cops. I don't see how I could trust you."

"But you could, absolutely. I couldn't tell anyone without incriminating myself, don't you see? I'd never say a word."

Robison crossed his arms and stared intently at Murphy for several seconds. He shook his head again.

"Suppose I could get you some of these 'diet pills,' could you meet me later with the cash? It's not like I have them here in my pocket. Can you have cash?"

"Oh, sure. Today's Friday — I just got paid. I'll be at *The Journal* office most of the night, but I could leave long enough to meet you. Where will you be?"

"Meet me in the alley next to Blackie's Tavern at eleven thirty. And be quiet about it. And bring fifty bucks."

When he got to the newspaper office, Murphy went to work in the stuffy darkroom that smelled strongly of photographic chemicals. He developed the roll of film and when it was dry printed some of the better shots from the football game.

He checked the clock and slipped out the front door, crossing the courthouse square to meet Robison. He was apprehensive, nervous about bringing cash, wondering if Robison would try something funny, but the transaction took only a moment. When Robison handed him the pill bottle, Murphy mumbled, "Thanks." Robison looked at him as if he had said something insane, then turned and disappeared into the darkness.

When Murphy returned to the office, Sox had arrived and soon turned in his account of the game. He helped Murphy with captions for the photos, identifying the players by their jersey numbers. It wasn't long until they heard the rumble of the press starting.

Murphy went back to the press room and helped a couple of part-time employees stuff advertising inserts into more than four thousand copies of the paper as they came off the press. Then the papers were run through the addressing machine, were tied in bundles and put into big canvas bags to be taken to the post office. It was three a.m. when he finally hung up his apron and went home.

For the first time in several nights, Murphy slept soundly, but at first light he awoke suddenly to the horrifying sensation of insects crawling all over his body. With a scream, he jumped off the bed, furiously scratching his arms, legs, belly — wherever he could reach. Not only could he feel the bugs *on* his skin, some seemed to be just *under* his skin. He didn't see any bugs, but he could definitely feel them.

"What the hell!" he cried, darting wildly around the room, alternately scratching and rubbing his limbs and even his head and face. His heart was pounding, and his left arm started to bleed where he had scratched it so violently.

Finally he ran into the bathroom, stripped, and got into the tub, lying back and letting the water run until it reached his chin. Gradually the feeling of being covered with moving insects subsided.

Luckily, since it was Saturday, he didn't have to go to work. After he was dressed and feeling somewhat more normal, he got a beer from the refrigerator and sat at the dining table. He opened the bottle Robison had sold him and dumped the rainbow colored pills on the table. He counted an even one hundred.

"That's good," he thought. "Once I start feeling better I can cut back gradually, over a two-month period instead of one month."

He took one of the pills, washing it down with beer. He thought about lying down but knew he couldn't sleep. He was also afraid the bug thing might come back.

He spent the rest of the day walking around town, killing time, visiting the public library, the town park, the cafe, and the small downtown grocery store. He stopped at the liquor store and bought a fifth of cheap bourbon.

Back at the apartment, he had just finished his dinner, which consisted of a slice of bologna and two slices of white bread, when there was a knock at the door.

For no reason he could think of, Murphy was immediately filled with a flurry of alarm and dread, but he steeled himself and went to the door. As he opened it he was relieved to find it was Mindy Gregor, his sometimes girlfriend. She was a petite young woman with long, straight blonde hair and granny glasses. She was wearing a tie-dyed tee shirt, jeans, and sandals.

She held up a four-pack of peach wine coolers,

saying, "I thought we could just hang out. Do you have to work or anything?"

"No, come on in," Murphy said. "I've got some whiskey, too."

While Mindy opened one of her wine coolers, Murphy put The Doors' *L.A. Woman* album on the record player and poured himself some bourbon over ice. They sat on the futon, enjoying the music, drinking and chatting. When he'd finished his drink, Murphy got up to pour another and pick out another album to play. When he turned around, Mindy stood up and pulled her shirt off over her head. She wasn't wearing a bra.

"C'mon," she said, smiling. She took his hand and led him into the bedroom. While Murphy undressed she shucked off her jeans, and they crawled into bed.

After several minutes of kissing and fondling, Mindy rose up on her elbow and asked, "Is something wrong, Murph?"

"I don't know," he said, "nothing's happening. This is weird! It's not that I don't *want* to; that's for damned sure. This isn't good. Shit! I just don't know."

He flopped onto his back and lay staring at the ceiling.

"Maybe I'm just really tired," he said. "I was up all night getting the paper out. That's the only thing I can think of to explain it. I'm sorry. This is really embarrassing."

"No, it's okay," she said. "We can still snuggle. Maybe you need to get some sleep."

Thanks to the pills and whiskey, the rest of the weekend went by in a blur. Murphy made it to work on time on Monday and spent the morning typing and working on content.

Just before lunch, Editor Davers stuck his head in the door and asked, "Can you get a picture of Denise Spurlin this afternoon over at her office? I need it for the Realtors Association layout I'm working on. It'd be nice to have it yet today or by tomorrow for sure."

"Yeah, I can do it," Murphy said.

"Might be a good time for you to try out the new film loader — you'll only need a few shots. Denise said she'd be at her office all afternoon, so you can go any time. Get something casual, relaxed; more than just a head shot."

"Okay," Murphy said as Davers headed back to his office. He went into the darkroom and loaded a short roll of film, which he put it into his Pentax K1000, a workhorse of a camera with few bells and whistles, although it did boast a built-in light meter.

Murphy knew who Denise Spurlin was. Everyone at the newspaper knew who she was. They were often present at the same community functions — awards banquets, ribbon cuttings, chamber of commerce programs. He couldn't claim she was a friend, really, just one of those people you would say "Hi" to around town.

When he got to her office later that afternoon, the "open" sign was in the window, so he went in. There was no receptionist, but Spurlin heard the door and came out of her office. They exchanged greetings and went right to work. He took shots of her at her desk, standing by a large bookcase holding some papers, and one by the open front door so he could use the natural light.

She was a pretty young woman and very photogenic, with dark curly hair that framed her face nicely. She was wearing a filmy silk flowered top under an extremely pale green jacket and matching flared skirt that ended just above her knees. Murphy couldn't help noticing how that skirt swirled around her shapely legs when she walked across the room.

As soon as they were through, he went back to the office and straight into the darkroom. In darkness, he took the film out of the camera and out of its spool and wound it onto a stainless steel reel that fit precisely into the developing tank. He put the lid on the tank and poured developer into it through a baffled opening on the top. Then he set the timer. He went back to his desk and typed until the timer bell rang. Back in the darkroom he poured off the developer and filled the tank with fixer. After the timer rang again, he could safely remove the lid and pour the fixer back into its container. He put the tank in the sink under the faucet and let water run through it for several minutes. When that was done, he dumped the water and filled the tank with something called Photo-flo™ so that when he removed the strip of film, squeegeed it off, and hung it up to dry there would be no water spots. He went back to his desk and worked until enough time had passed for the film to be dry to the touch.

Now it was time to see what he got in the photo shoot.

He slid the film strip into the negative carrier and inserted that into the vertical enlarger. When he flipped a switch, the enlarger's light would shine down through the negative and project the image onto an adjustable easel lying flat on the enlarger base. Moveable black metal arms on the easel allowed him to choose the size of print he would make. Once everything was focused and sized, he would turn off the enlarger, insert a sheet of photo paper into the easel, and hit a timer that would activate the enlarger light for a specified number of seconds.

"Whoa!" he muttered suddenly. He moved the film until the next frame was projected.

"What the hell!"

He moved to the next frame.

"Oh, no!"

He took the film strip out of the enlarger and turned on the overhead light. He held the film up and examined it from end to end. He began to panic. Every frame had a wide black swath right through its center, wiping out most of the image.

"What? No, no, no!" he moaned, walking in circles, holding up the damaged film. "This can't be! Not possible! No, no, no!"

He felt as if he wanted to cry or scream or throw things. The film was ruined! Somewhere along the way — from first loading the roll of film and putting it in the camera, to all the steps of the developing process — at some point, somehow, light had gotten to the film. There was no going back, the damage was permanent, no way to recover the images — they were gone, obliterated.

Murphy felt he was going to be sick but choked back the bile. He pounded his fist against the edge of the big sink.

"Aarghh!" Wild-eyed, he scanned the ceiling as if the answer could be there. He looked at the piece of film again and then angrily threw it into the trashcan.

He continued to pace, but more slowly now, gradually regaining some composure. Given what had happened, he realized, there was only one thing he could do: retake the pictures. He'd have to call Denise and explain. Hopefully, he could go get some new shots and be back before Davers even knew what happened. Murphy didn't want to sit through a lecture about loading the film carefully. He knew all that. Whatever had happened was a complete fluke.

When he called, Denise was as gracious as ever.

"That's alright, John," she said after he explained. "Come back over, and we'll run through it again."

Since they were repeating the same poses they had done only an hour earlier, this session went quickly. But after he had taken the final shot of her standing in the soft light from the doorway, she startled him by stepping closer and placing her left hand on his shoulder. Then, even more astonishing, she moved in, looked up into his eyes and kissed him. It was an intense, passionate, lingering kiss, and he could feel the warm contours of her body pressed hard against him as her lips moved against his and her tongue probed insistently.

Then, just as suddenly, she stepped back and said brightly, "So, have you got everything you need?"

Murphy's head was still spinning, but he managed, "Yeah. Um, yeah. We're all set. Sorry about the re-do."

She had already started toward her inner office. "No problem," she called back over her shoulder. "Thanks!"

Back in the darkroom, Murphy carefully worked through each step of the developing process as if it were his first time. When at last he hung the film up to dry he was enormously relieved to see a sequence of healthy-looking negatives.

When the film was dry he printed a couple of the shots he thought were best. Working under a safelight, which cast an eerie red glow over the room, he used the enlarger to project the image onto a sheet of photo paper. Then he slid the paper into a tray containing developer, using tongs to be sure it was completely submerged. He watched as the image magically began to appear, faint at first but slowly becoming clearer. It was the shot of Denise at her desk. When it was fully developed, he moved the paper to the next tray, containing stop bath, for just a few seconds, and then into the final tray, which held the fixer. He also printed the shot of Denise standing in the soft, flattering light from the doorway. They looked good. Davers could pick the one he wanted to use in his layout.

Murphy removed the negative strip from the enlarger and was starting to file it away when he noticed something odd. There appeared to be an image on the last frame in the strip that wasn't part of the sequence with Denise. He couldn't tell what it was.

He put the film back into the enlarger, moved it through to that final frame, slid in a sheet of paper and exposed it. He slipped the paper into the developer tray and gently swirled the liquid with the tongs. Slowly the image began to appear, but it was still a mystery.

"I didn't take this," he said under his breath.

As the image grew more vivid, he realized it was a horizontal photo, but he was looking at it vertically, so he turned the tray and watched in growing horror as it reached full clarity.

"Oh," he whispered. "Oh. No. What? This can't be. No. Oh, my God!"

The black-and-white photo showed a woman lying in a pool of blood.

"Denise? That can't be; it's not possible! Where did this come from? I didn't take this!"

But it *was* Denise lying there. Her lipstick was smeared across her cheek, the filmy silk blouse ripped away, her skirt hiked up around her hips. Her lifeless eyes were staring straight into the camera.

Murphy staggered away from the sink and fell back against the darkroom door. He put both hands to his head and squeezed his temples. Surely he was losing his mind. There was no way that picture could exist. Denise isn't dead.

Then it occurred to him that he couldn't let anyone else see the print. If they didn't put him in prison, they'd put him in a mental hospital for sure.

He had moved it from the developer to the fixer. Now he put it in the sink and let clean water wash over it for a few minutes. Trying not to look directly at the horrifying image, he used a stack of paper towels to blot it until it felt merely damp. Then he grabbed an empty eight by ten paper box and put the picture in that.

He hid the box under his shirt and quickly made his way through and out of the office. He hurried across the courthouse square and practically ran across the street to his apartment.

Once inside, he put the box on top of his bookshelf, out of sight. He took one of his pills and spent the rest of the evening trying to drink enough whiskey to erase the terrifying image from his mind.

The next morning Murphy could barely drag himself out of bed. He avoided even looking at the bright yellow box on top of the bookshelf. After a trip to the bathroom, he came back into the kitchen feeling shaky and weak. He opened a beer, took one of his pills, and sat on the futon looking out the front window, idly watching people coming and going at the courthouse.

At one point, three sheriff's cars pulled in and flat parked in front. Three uniformed officers got out and stood talking on the sidewalk. For a moment he wondered if they could be talking about him but then decided that wasn't likely. There was no way they could know about the insane photograph, and if Bud had squealed about selling him pills that would be a case for the town cop, not the sheriff's department. After a little while two of the deputies got back into their cars and drove away. The third went into the courthouse.

He thought about calling in sick but didn't know what he would do all day if he didn't go to work.

He barely got to his desk before Davers came rushing in. "You're late!" he hissed. "Didn't you hear what happened?"

Murphy shook his head no. "What?"

"There's been a murder," Davers said excitedly. Murphy felt a cold sense of dread forming in his chest. "Somebody killed Denise Spurlin at her office. You need to get over there, get some pictures — you know, cops going in and out of her office, that sort of thing."

Murphy gripped the edge of his desk and clenched his jaw, trying not to lose control, trying not to scream.

"When did this happen?" he managed to ask.

"Sometime during the night," Davers said. "They found her this morning." He noticed how pale Murphy had become and added, "I'm sorry. This has to be a shock for you since you were just over there yesterday.

We're all stunned. Can't imagine who could have done it or why. Everyone liked her."

He turned to go back to his office. "Well, soon as you pull yourself together you need to go cover the scene. Talk to people in the other offices, see if they saw or heard anything — you know the drill. We'll need everything for tonight's press run."

The rest of the day Murphy put his mind on autopilot, taking photos and interviewing businesspeople in the office complex where Denise had worked. Even though all said they had not seen or heard anything unusual, their comments still would make a news story when strung together with the who, what, where and when of the sheriff's department press release.

He was relieved when no inexplicable images showed up on the film he developed.

At dinnertime he took a break long enough to go to his apartment and eat a bologna sandwich. The box was still on top of the bookcase, undisturbed. He took one of his pills and went back to help get the paper out.

Local Realtor Murdered, the front page headline screamed. The report carried Murphy's byline and was accompanied by two photos: uniformed cops carrying a cardboard box from her office, presumably some sort of evidence, and the sheriff speaking at his press conference. So far, he said, there were no suspects.

It was nearly three a.m. when all the papers were addressed, bagged, and taken to the post office. By the time Murphy got to his apartment he was so exhausted he sat at the dining table, held his head in his hands, and wept.

He woke up in bed the next morning with the furious sensation of insects crawling all over his skin. Before he was fully awake he had scratched his face, drawing blood. Shaking and swatting his chest and arms, he hurried to the tub and, as it filled, leaned back, gritted his teeth, and tried not to scratch as the water rose to his chin.

When the attack had subsided he dressed and went to the kitchen. He fixed himself a bowl of cold cereal, but when he started to eat discovered his hand was trembling so much he couldn't get the spoon from the bowl to his mouth without shaking off the milk and cereal. Bracing his right hand with his left, he managed to finish. Then he took one of his pills and headed off to work.

The next two days were uneventful, filled with routine work followed by nights of pills and alcohol. Although once, during his lunch break, he was sitting on a bench in front of the courthouse steps drinking a Coke, when he saw two women talking inside the hardware store across the street. Even though he knew it should be impossible, he could hear every word they were saying as clearly as if he were standing next to them.

"Surely it's someone from out of town," one of them said. "No one from Riverton would do such a horrible thing."

"I hope you're right," the other one said. "But why? Why would anyone hurt Denise? She was such a nice young woman. I can't imagine anyone hating her enough to murder her!"

Murphy put his drink down on the bench and covered his ears with his hands, but he could still hear their simpering comments. Finally he leapt up and went back to the office to work.

Friday night brought the opening game of the post-season football playoffs. As he walked across town to the stadium, Murphy found he could once again hear conversations taking place inside homes along the way. Only once did someone mention the murder investigation, repeating a detail Murphy had reported in *The Journal*. He found the rest of the talk boring and stupid. He had no idea how or why he was hearing all of it and wished it would stop.

The weekend flew by in a blur of pills and alcohol. Mindy stopped by once and made scrambled eggs and toast, insisting he eat something.

"You look like hell," she said, frowning. "Your face is gaunt, you've got scabs on your cheeks, big dark circles under your eyes. I'm worried about you, Murph!"

She didn't stay long.

Monday afternoon Murphy was in his cubicle typing up miscellaneous news items when Davers came in.

"Got another photo chore for you," he said. "Go over to the depot and get a picture of Louie Cockerham with his plaque. He's been named engineer of the year or some stupid-ass thing. Just get enough for a photo and cutline; it's not worth a big feature story. He's there now, if you can go."

The railroader was tall and lanky with light brown hair sprinkled with gray. He held up his award for Murphy to see.

"I know it's not a big deal," he said, "but my wife insisted on calling the paper. She's proud of it."

"Well, of course," Murphy said. He took down some information about the award and then suggested, "Why don't we step outside for the photo? We won't have to worry about having enough light. I'd rather not use a flash."

The depot was at the east edge of town, and just beyond the building was a steep drop-off that went down to the river. A bridge carried the tracks over the huge ravine. A deck at the rear of the building overlooked the scene.

"If you hold the plaque up so the top of it is just to the right of your chin, I can get in nice and close," Murphy directed. He snapped a shot, checked the metering again, and took another.

"What do you hear about the murder investigation?" Cockerham asked. "The sheriff have any idea who did it?"

"Apparently not," Murphy said. "There hasn't been much to report."

"Well, you can bet it's someone we all know."

"What do you mean?"

"This is a small town, Murph. Everybody knows everybody else. So when they find out who it is, we're all gonna know them."

He took a dark brown cigarillo out of his shirt pocket and lit it with an old Zippo.

"You know how it is on the news when they arrest someone for something like this. The townspeople all say, 'He was quiet and kept to himself. Never caused any trouble.' It's always the last person you would suspect."

He exhaled a stream of odorous smoke. "Hell, it could be me. It could even be you, Murph!"

Murphy's face grew dark. "What do you mean by that?"

"I don't mean anything. Just that it could be anybody, you know?"

"Well, it's not you, and it's not me, and you shouldn't go around saying stuff like that. Someone might take you seriously."

"Nobody's that stupid," Cockerham laughed. "But mark my words: when they catch him it'll be someone we all know." He flipped the cigarillo over the deck railing and watched it sail through the air to the rugged rocks far below.

The man's remark had unnerved him, but Murphy tried to convince himself it hadn't meant anything as he made his way back to the office.

When he developed the short roll of film he had

loaded for the assignment, he wasn't taken by surprise when he saw an extra frame that didn't belong. He had been expecting this to happen again and hoping against hope that it wouldn't. Still, he trembled, gripping the edge of the darkroom sink as he watched the developer bring up the printed image.

"Jesus," he whispered. "What's going on?"

The extra photograph showed the train engineer's lifeless body lying across the rocks at the bottom of the ravine behind the depot. The rocks were stained black with the blood from Cockerham's fractured skull.

But it's insane, Murphy thought frantically. He knew for a fact that Cockerham was alive and well. But for how long, he wondered.

When Mindy stopped by his apartment that night, she was shocked by how bad Murphy looked. He seemed frail and weak when he moved around the apartment, and she noticed how his hand shook when he reached for the beer he used to wash down his pills. His eyes were red-rimmed as if he hadn't slept for days, and there were deep, half-healed scratches on his face and arms.

"You don't look well at all, Murph," she said. "You need to see Dr. Ellis."

Murphy shook his head. "I'm alright. I've just been working hard. With that murder and everything. It's gotten on my nerves, and I haven't slept much."

He sat with his elbows on his knees, wringing his hands. "There's some crazy stuff going on. This film

Davers bought . . . I can't explain it. It's like it captures images of things that haven't even happened yet. I can't explain it. It doesn't make any sense, but it's like it sees the future."

"Maybe you should take it to the race track," Mindy said lightly. "We could make a killing on the horses if it shows us who's going to win."

"It's not a joke," Murphy snapped. "It's crazy, but it's happening."

Mindy grew serious again. "I don't think those pills are good for you," she said. "They make you jumpy and could even be the reason you can't sleep. And you definitely don't need to lose any more weight — you're thin as a rail. You don't look healthy."

"Well, I'm fine!" he barked. "I don't need to see Dr. Ellis. He doesn't know what I need. These pills give me energy. And I'm only taking them through the end of the month; I'm going to start tapering off."

"I read an article in *Readers' Digest* about some of the side effects they're finding out about," she said earnestly. "And one was exactly what happened — or didn't happen — between us the other night."

"Bullshit!" He blushed furiously. "That was a one-time thing because I'd worked 20 hours straight. Nothing to do with pills. You never had any complaints before."

"I'm not complaining now, Murph. I'm just worried about you. There were other things, too — paranoia, something called 'auditory hallucinations' like people thinking they could hear voices even through walls, people scratching and picking at their skin, loss of sleep — even homicidal thoughts. I'm really worried about you."

He sat without speaking, shaking his head, looking down at his hands.

She gathered her things and went to the door. "Please at least think about seeing the doctor," she said. Then she left, quietly closing the door behind her.

When Murphy came down the stairs from his apartment the next morning and opened the door to the street, he could see the sheriff's car parked in front of the newspaper office. Suddenly he was filled with apprehension. He assumed the sheriff was talking to Davers, and he wondered if they were talking about him. He waited, just inside the door, peeking out occasionally, until the sheriff came out, got in his vehicle and drove away. It had been almost forty-five minutes.

He had barely stepped inside the front office when Davers barked, "You're late!"

Murphy headed for his cubicle with Davers on his heels.

"There's been another death," the editor said. "Louie Cockerham, at the depot. Another coincidence, with you being there just yesterday."

Murphy's heart was pounding. He gripped the arms of his desk chair and fought to control his breathing. "What happened?" he asked.

"He fell from the deck behind the depot down into that big ravine and landed on the rocks. They don't know yet if it was an accident or if he was pushed. It seems suspicious, though, coming right after what happened to Denise. Either way, it'll make a page one story."

Davers looked at his watch. "Since you weren't here, I sent Sox over to the scene. He'll need you to develop his film when he gets back."

Left on his own, Murphy tried to process the terrible news, but the black-and-white images of the two victims swirled around in his mind like an out of control movie projector.

Later that afternoon, the sports editor, excited about the chance to write a front page news story, turned his copy in to Davers.

"You gave the film to Murphy, right?" Davers asked. Sox said he did, and Davers said, "I'll go by and see what he came up with."

He went down the hall to Murphy's cubicle, but the reporter wasn't at his desk. The door to the darkroom was open, so Davers assumed it was safe to go in. As he approached he heard a soft mewling, whimpering sound. Frowning, he pushed open the door. The room was bathed in the safelight's red glow.

As his eyes adjusted, Davers saw a figure huddled in the corner between the sink and the wall.

"Murphy?"

Now he could hear soft sobbing. The person's

shoulders were shaking convulsively. Davers started toward him but then noticed a print floating in the tray of fixer.

"What the hell is that?" he muttered. "What on earth?"

It appeared to be a photograph of a person being executed in the electric chair. The man was strapped in the heavy wooden chair, obviously being subjected to the deadly jolt of electricity just as the image was captured. His body was arched upward and rigid, straining against the unyielding straps. On his head there was a battered leather cap with an electrode on top connected to a power cord. A faint wisp of smoke was coming from the connection. The cap was affixed with a chin strap, making it resemble an old fashioned football helmet. The man's teeth were bared in a hideous grimace, his skin pulled tight over his cheekbones. His eyes were open wide in terror.

"My God," Davers whispered, grasping the edge of the sink to steady himself.

The man in the chair was John Murphy.

Lizzy's Day

The first time Lizzy saw John Taulbee he was galloping past her father's sharecropper cabin on a spirited black stallion. Lizzy had just turned sixteen. A week later at a neighborhood barn dance, John took her by the hand, led her into the tobacco patch behind the barn, and kissed her on the lips. Three months later they were married. They moved into Indiana, where John purchased a tract of land near the river. He contracted with a lumber company to supply poplar, white oak, and walnut logs, which he floated down the river to the mill.

Lizzy had been attracted to Taulbee's good looks, easy smile, and constant concern for her every desire or whim. But things changed dramatically after they were married and set up housekeeping in a remote little cabin.

On this particular winter afternoon, Lizzy was scurrying around the kitchen, hoping to put together a supper that would please her husband and to have it ready the moment he returned from his day's work. She had roasted a chicken with potatoes and carrots, and there were fresh biscuits and, for dessert, an apple crumble.

Her tension increased when she heard him approaching, and a moment later John Taulbee burst through the door. She was placing plates and forks on the table, and her back was to the door. He strode across the room, pressed himself against her, and reached under her arm to seize her breast.

"I been thinkin' about this all day," he growled. He put a hand on the back of her neck and shoved her face down onto the table. Hiking her skirts to her waist, he forced himself into her, pounding viciously until he made a final shuddering thrust, then withdrew, slapping her buttock and laughing.

"That ought to hold you for a while," he said with a sneer. Lizzy still had her back to him, trying to adjust her clothes. Grabbing her shoulder he spun her to face him, and when he saw the tears in her eyes his scowl drew dark and he slapped her face. "You useless whore!" he bellowed. He shoved her toward the open fireplace, causing her to stumble across the room. "Get over there and get my supper on the table or I'll give you something to cry about!"

He ate his meal in silence while Lizzy hovered in the background, relieved that the food seemed to suit him. Only when he left the table and went outside did she prepare her own plate.

Taulbee had a small pot bellied stove in the barn, and many evenings he would sit drinking whisky and smoking his corncob pipe until bedtime. When he didn't return to the cabin for a while, Lizzy assumed he was following his usual routine. She was thankful for the brief respite but fearful of how the whisky might affect his temper.

After a time she changed quickly into her night-dress and crawled into bed, drawing the comforter up to her chin and feigning sleep. She lay like that for what seemed an eternity, listening for his return and praying he would not force himself on her again.

At last she heard the door open and close and listened as he stumbled around the room. Then he sat on a creaking chair and took off his boots. She held her breath as he slipped beneath the covers. She smelled a mix of whisky and tobacco and sweat. But within minutes he was snoring loudly, and she breathed a tiny sigh of relief. She lay awake for hours, thinking about the torment her life had become and whether she would ever find a way to escape.

Lizzy was up before dawn. She stoked the fire, put on the coffee and the biscuits, and started frying bacon. When the bacon and biscuits were done, she cracked five eggs into the skillet of hot bacon grease just as she heard her husband starting to stir. He pulled on his boots and went to the washstand in the corner. He splashed some water on his face and came to the table just as Lizzy slid three of the fried eggs onto a plate. The remaining two would be for her.

She placed his food and mug of hot coffee on the table as he sat down. He took a biscuit and snarled, "These biscuits is cold!" But he wolfed down his breakfast, biscuits and all, and finished his coffee.

As he stood, Taulbee suddenly grabbed Lizzy by the hair and jerked her close to him. She tried to keep the terror from showing on her face. "Sometimes I wonder why I even keep you around here," he muttered. "Lord knows you're about as worthless as teats on a boar hog."

She grew pale as he drew his pistol and held the barrel against her temple. "You know, one of these days I might take a notion to just *kill* you," he said. "I could toss your body in that river and nobody would ever know. 'Fore long I could go to the city and get me a real good-lookin' woman, and nobody'd ever know the difference. You sure wouldn't be missed."

He shoved her away and crossed to the door, stopping to put on his hat, coat, and gloves. "You bring me something decent to eat straight up at noon," he ordered. "Don't mess it up." He gave a cruel laugh. "You never know — today might be the day!"

The door closed behind him, and she stood leaning on the table, her shoulders shaking as she sobbed in despair.

Axe in hand, Taulbee followed the path along the river to his work site, marked by numerous large tree stumps and several long, straight logs lying on the frozen ground. Once the spring thaw broke up the ice on the river he would have a good supply of logs to float down to the sawmill.

His father had taught him that a razor sharp axe made the work go easier and faster, and he always kept his tools well honed. He picked out a huge poplar tree and began cutting a notch on the side toward the river. Each blow of the axe sent a large wood chip flying. Soon he had opened a notch across and almost halfway through the thick tree trunk at a point little more than a foot above ground.

Taulbee rested for a few minutes and then grabbed his one-man crosscut saw. He set it about a foot higher on the opposite side of the tree and began sawing at a downward angle. The new cut would eventually meet the notch at its deepest point in the trunk. More than likely the tree would begin to lean and fall even before he cut all the way through.

Gradually the cut deepened as it neared the lower notch, but the tree continued to stand tall and straight. Suddenly there was a loud "crack!" Taulbee withdrew the saw and looked up along the trunk of the towering tree. Something wasn't right. Slowly the huge trunk began to twirl on its stump, giving no clue as to which way it might fall. Taulbee dropped the saw and ran but had gone only a few yards when a stubborn greenbriar caught his ankle. He fell face first onto the hard ground. He rolled onto his back just in time to see the gigantic tree coming down with a deafening crash. The trunk struck him across the chest, knocking the wind out of him. But amazingly, he was still alive.

Gradually his breath returned. After the initial

impact, the trunk had risen slightly, buoyed by the branches of its crown. It no longer pressed against his chest. He realized that crown had saved his life, preventing the trunk from crushing his rib cage and lungs. His hands were free on either side of his body, and he felt beneath his back and buttocks to see if he could scrape aside any soil to create more breathing space between the tree trunk and his chest or even to allow him to squirm out from under the tree. But his fingers were no match for the hard-packed, icy dirt. Then he heard a popping sound farther along the log and felt it drop a little closer. Each time a branch snapped the trunk settled a little more.

Taulbee cried out in fear and frustration, clawing furiously at the soil alongside his body and trying to move his hips to one side or the other, all to no avail. Another branch cracked, and he felt the rough bark of the tree trunk touch his chest.

When the sun had risen straight overhead, Lizzy walked along the path from the cabin carrying a basket containing a wedge of cheese, bacon left over from breakfast, two biscuits, and an apple as well as a corked bottle containing switchel, a thirst-quenching mixture of water, honey, and vinegar. She was reluctant to hurry, knowing Taulbee's reaction to her arrival could be unpleasant, and yet she knew that being late would definitely spark his wrath.

She arrived at the work site where several large

logs, trimmed of all branches, lay awaiting the trip down the river. She wound her way through scattered stumps and piles of brush, looking for Taulbee, puzzled that she could not see him or hear any chopping or sawing. She gasped when, finally, she saw his boots and legs on the ground, sticking out from under a massive poplar log. She walked to the end of the tree trunk and back up the other side until she saw his head barely clear of the curve of the log. She approached and looked down at him.

"Lizzy!" he cried. "Thank God! You've got to save me! Run back to the house and get a shovel — maybe you can dig me out before this log settles and crushes me to death!"

She walked along the tree trunk, appraising the situation, looking at the crown and noticing how some of the smaller branches had already snapped.

"Lizzy, help me!" Taulbee shouted hoarsely. "Go get a shovel!"

She walked back to where he lay. "You seem to have gotten yourself into quite a pickle, John," she said calmly. "I don't think you could count on a useless whore to get you out of there. I don't believe I could dig you out — I'm not strong enough."

"Lizzy, goddamn it!" he shouted.

She strolled over to a large stump and sat. She took the piece of cheese from the basket and took a bite, then a bite of bread, and washed them down with a gulp of switchel.

"Lizzy! For God's sake! You've got to help me! Go saddle my horse and ride to town. Bring back four or five men. Hurry!" Taulbee's cries were punctuated by a sharp cracking sound as another branch collapsed and the log settled another quarter inch, pressing on his chest.

Lizzy nibbled cheese and bread. "Why, John, I'm surprised at you," she said. "You know the rules — I'm not allowed to go anywhere near that fine horse of yours. Remember what you said you'd do to me if I ever tried? No, I don't believe I could do that."

"Lizzy," Taulbee sobbed. "I'm sorry if I was unkind to you. Maybe I made you hate me. But you've got to get help! I'm going to die here!"

She stood and picked up the basket. "That may be, John," she said. "But there's not much I can do about it. I'll tell you what, though, I'll come back about supper time and see how you're doing." She started walking back toward the house.

"Lizzy! Please, Lizzy! For the love of God!" Taulbee sobbed.

Soon she was far enough down the path that she could no longer hear him.

Back at the cabin Lizzy went about preparing supper as usual, although she had decided to keep the meal simple: a bit of boiled beef and unpeeled potatoes roasted in the coals of the fireplace. To pass the time she sat in the rocking chair and read her Bible. In Isaiah she found, *"Thus I will punish the world for its evil. And the wicked for their iniquity; I will also put an end to the arrogance of the proud and abase the haughtiness of the ruthless."* She took it as a sign and nodded in silent agreement. Her husband was an arrogant, cruel, and ruthless man, deserving of punishment, which had come in the form of a God-given poplar tree.

At the usual supper hour she bundled some of the beef and a potato and put the food into the basket. She put on her wrap and headed down the path to the logging site. She made her way to the fallen poplar and the body of her husband. She knew he was dead. His skin was a pale bluish-gray, and his darkened tongue protruded slightly.

"I reckon the branches didn't hold," she said quietly.

She walked back to the cabin and ate her supper, followed by the last of the apple crumble from the day before and a rare cup of hot tea.

After the meal she heated water and bathed, drying off in front of the open fireplace. She had no large mirror in which to assess her naked body but felt certain her charms had not faded significantly — after all, she was only twenty years old.

Dressed in her nightgown, she padded about the cabin, putting clothing and a few keepsakes into a faded old carpetbag. At sunup she dressed in her warmest winter clothes. She gathered her belongings and went to the barn where she saddled the sleek black horse and rode off to find a new life in the nearest town.

Henry And The
Night Sky

*"I can calculate the motion of heavenly bodies
but not the madness of people."*
—*Isaac Newton*

H enry wasn't surprised when Vera began to complain about living in the country. She had reluctantly agreed they should purchase the property after he repeatedly explained what a great deal it was. They were getting twenty acres of rolling pasture with scattered clumps of large trees, a barn, and a modern A-frame house overlooking a small lake — all for less than half the cost of a tiny bungalow in the city. Because Henry was an accountant, Vera grudgingly accepted his opinions when it came to financial matters. Sometimes he felt it was the only area in which she didn't consider him incompetent.

They made the move immediately after his retirement from the megabank at Indianapolis where he had spent thirty-five years, surviving a variety of mergers and acquisitions without calling attention to himself. Members of his department whisked him off to a bar at the end of his final day at the bank, bought him a drink, and presented him with a rustic "welcome" plaque to hang outside his new home, which his co-workers persistently referred to as a "cabin" despite his efforts to describe its amenities.

The bank honored Henry, along with several dozen other employees, at the annual service awards banquet, and his picture was published in the company newsletter with a brief caption noting his years of service. "Henry and his wife, Vera, will spend their golden years on a farm about sixty-five miles south of Indianapolis," the newsletter stated. Henry felt the writer's use of the word "farm" was inaccurate but decided it was not an error worth correcting.

During the first few weeks they were occupied with the process of "settling in" to their new home, but it took only a few days for Henry to discover his favorite spot — a small wooden deck overlooking the lake. Sitting on that deck in the late afternoon, listening to the birds' chatter, watching the mutable surface of the pond as the breeze rippled the water, and passing clouds constantly changed its color, he found a sense of peace and well-being he had not experienced for many years, if ever. Several times he encouraged Vera to join him, but she refused, citing the heat, or the insects, or the breeze that might disturb her hair, and after a while Henry stopped inviting her.

Even as Henry's love of the countryside grew, Vera's complaints about their new lifestyle became more vocal.

"I don't have any friends here," she lamented, sitting in their formal dining room, sipping tea from a delicate china cup. "There's nothing to do here; it's boring and depressing."

"Now, Vera," Henry explained patiently, "I've told you — they have a very active community theater group in town; you could get involved in that. They have an arts and crafts center; you could get involved in that and make some new friends. Why, there's even a local women's group that helps drum up support for the Indianapolis Symphony."

But Vera would have none of it, although she seemed placated somewhat when Henry reminded her that they could jump in the car and be in Indianapolis in little over an hour if she wanted to attend a concert or a play or meet with the women's committee at the art museum.

"And besides," he added, "you can visit by telephone any time," as if he weren't aware that was exactly how she had been spending most of her days since they moved. From what he could gather, her side of those conversations consisted mostly of detailed accounts of her distaste for rural life.

One evening Henry went out to his deck after dinner and, as he sat and watched the sun slowly disappearing behind a distant row of smoky blue hills, he was so relaxed that he fell asleep in his lawn chair. When he awoke, darkness had fallen, but the night air was still warm and pleasant. As he leaned back and studied the sky he began to marvel at what he saw.

"It's so busy!" he thought to himself. Off to his right he could see the lights of a jetliner and hear its powerful engines as it worked its way across the sky from west to east. At the same time, another plane, too high to be heard, was passing directly overhead, probably en route from Indianapolis to Louisville. From moment to moment, in almost every direction, both high and low, the blinking lights of various craft continually plied the night sky. "I had no idea," Henry whispered.

Then he focused on the moon, which, at its fullest stage, had risen above the wooded ridge and now loomed impossibly close, its scars and craters clearly visible. Henry was fascinated. He realized he had not really looked at the moon and the stars for nearly 40 years. "In the city you can't see the sky at night because of the streetlights and all the other manmade lighting," he thought.

He noticed several stars — or planets; he didn't know which was which — that appeared to be larger and brighter than others and was annoyed that he couldn't identify them. He remembered as a child standing with his mother in the back yard as she pointed out the Big Dipper, and he turned now in his chair, searching the sky for that familiar outline. Eventually he located some stars that seemed to be in the right formation, but he couldn't be sure.

The next morning, Henry waited impatiently for the hardware store on Main Street to open. It was his first visit to the establishment, which had a small sign on its front door boasting "family owned for 70 years." As he opened the door, setting off a jingling bell, he felt as if he had stepped back in time.

The long, narrow building was packed, floor to ceiling, with merchandise, from tiny packets holding a few screws to large wheelbarrows, bicycles, kerosene lanterns, water heaters and lawnmowers. Henry gazed in wonder as he walked over the floor of narrow boards, heavily oiled, with shiny nailheads worn by years of foot traffic showing through here and there.

He strolled through aisles displaying electric fixtures, plumbing supplies, air rifles and fishing gear, baseball bats and gloves, racks filled with packets of garden seeds, shovels, rakes, hoes, hammers, saws, axes, and other tools, coils of rope and chain in various sizes, and a wall of bins holding bulk quantities of all sizes of nails, screws, nuts and bolts. Another wall was devoted to cans of paint in various colors and finishes, varnish, stains, brushes, rollers and other painters' accouterments.

An object hanging from one of the center posts supporting the ceiling caught Henry's eye. "Eliminate weeds without harsh chemicals," the cardboard packaging proclaimed. Fastened to the backing was a long hose made of some sturdy-looking black woven material with a metal snout at one end. Illustrations on the backing showed it was made to attach to a tank of propane gas. Then it could be used to direct flame onto unwanted weeds and grass. Drawings showed the "flame thrower" in action as well as the wilted, shriveled weeds destroyed by the intense heat.

"That would be just the thing for the weeds that grow up between the tire tracks in my gravel driveway," Henry thought.

His explorations were interrupted when a gray haired man with a slight limp approached and asked, "May I help you?"

"This is quite a place you have here," Henry beamed. "I hadn't been in before."

"Yep, "the man said. "If we ain't got it, you don't need it."

Both chuckled, and then the man asked, "What can I help you with?"

"I'm looking for a telescope," Henry said. "One powerful enough that I can look at the moon and the stars."

"Well, we get more call for binoculars, spotting scopes and rifle scopes for hunters," the man explained, but I seem to recall seeing a big telescope way back in the other room there."

He headed for the other side of the store with Henry trailing close behind. In the other room there were materials for repairing window screens, shelves filled with insecticides, herbicides and garden fertilizers, and in a far corner — behind some rolls of chicken wire and metal fence posts – a tall cardboard box with a picture of a telescope printed on it. The outdated style of the illustration and the heavy layer of dust on the box suggested it had been in that corner for a long time.

The man pulled the box out from behind the other merchandise and handed it to Henry.

"I believe this might be what you're looking for," he said.

Printing on the box indicated it was an "Equatorial Reflector Telescope" and promised it could be used to "view the Moon, the rings of Saturn and the moons of Jupiter."

"Also great for Terrestrial use!" another line trumpeted.

"Oh, this is great — this is just what I need," Henry told the man.

The telescope came with a sturdy wooden tripod and a booklet with maps of the night sky. Henry hurried home, set up the telescope on his deck, and then fussed and fidgeted away the afternoon until, at last, darkness came.

He spent the first two hours studying the moon's rugged face. Then, with the help of his maps, Henry found Venus hovering in the western sky and then the red-orange planet Mars in the southwest, approaching the bright star Antares in the constellation Scorpius. And he squealed with excitement when, an hour after midnight, he finally focused on the magnificent sight of Saturn and its tilted rings. He sat transfixed, peering into the eyepiece of the telescope, making occasional small adjustments, following the planets in their eternal dance across the heavens. When at last he realized it was almost dawn, he tore himself away and tiptoed into the house.

During the next several weeks, Henry became immersed in the same nightly routine, much to Vera's dismay. As soon as dinner ended, he would hurry out to his deck and wait for darkness to reveal the awesome splendor of the night sky. On occasions when rain and clouds drove him inside, Vera pretended to read a magazine but stole concerned glances from time to time as Henry flipped through TV channels, tried unsuccessfully to read the newspaper, went to the window and looked out, sighed, and returned to his recliner, only to keep repeating the ritual until bedtime.

It was on one of those rainy nights when Vera's concerns took a new and alarming direction. She glanced up from her reading and did a double take. Henry was not reading the newspaper but a magazine with a familiar name and a photograph of a half-naked woman on the cover.

"Henry! What on earth is that?" she gasped.

Henry looked at her and then turned the magazine in his hands to look at the cover as if he had forgotten its title. "It's *Playboy*," he replied.

"I know what it is!" Vera hissed. "It's a dirty magazine. Why on earth would you bring something like that into our home?" When he failed to respond, she continued: "I swear, these last few weeks I'm beginning to wonder if I know you at all. Have you been hiding some horrible perversion from me all these years?"

Henry closed the magazine again and looked at Vera over the rims of his glasses. "If you must know," he sighed, "I saw it on the newsstand, and I thought this article looked interesting. According to this, younger people are starting to discover things that were popular in the 1940s and '50s — things like good cigars and dry martinis. Like Sinatra and the Rat Pack. I thought it was interesting."

"What possible interest could you have in cigars and martinis?" she asked.

"My father smoked cigars," Henry said softly, staring off into space. "I remember how they smelled — like leather and cedar and cured tobacco all mixed together. When my father walked into a room those aromas and the fragrance of that old green Mennen aftershave would precede him. I always thought it was a good smell. It was reassuring to know he was there."

Vera gave him a long, hard look.

"Well, when you're through reading, just get that trash out of here," she said. "I'd die if anyone saw it."

The next day Henry went into the local liquor store and bought a fifth of gin, a bottle of dry vermouth, a jar of olives, a cocktail shaker, and two martini glasses. Then he went to the tobacco shop and bought ten long-filler cigars, hand-rolled in the Dominican Republic. He chose the impressive "Churchill" size — seven inches long and a hefty 50-ring diameter. The clerk also pointed out that he would need a cutter to snip the ends of the cigars before lighting them. Henry remembered seeing his father bite off the tip of a cigar and spit out the little piece of tobacco as he prepared to light up, but Henry purchased the small guillotine cutter recommended by the clerk, along with a butane lighter.

Vera, of course, was not pleased when she walked into the kitchen that evening to prepare dinner and found Henry pouring his first martini into one of the funnel-shaped cocktail glasses.

"Ah, Vera!" Henry exclaimed, turning and raising his glass. "May I pour you a martini?"

Vera stood silent for a moment, a frightened expression on her face. Then she turned and stomped angrily from the room.

"No, thank you, Henry," Henry murmured in a Vera-like falsetto. He took a sip of his martini and then bowed and extended his glass as if joining a companion in a toast. "Don't you have anything stronger, Henry?"

On this evening he awaited the arrival of darkness with a martini in his left hand and a cigar in his right, the fragrant smoke swirling around his head before being caught by the breeze and snatched around the corner of the house. The spicy bite of the gin seemed a perfect foil for the earthy nuttiness of the cigar. As he sat in his deck chair with his feet up and his head back, he wondered why he had discovered these pleasures so late in life.

And the evening became even more wondrous after midnight as Henry reveled in the spectacle of the Perseid meteor shower, the number of sightings increasing in the early morning hours as the Earth's rotation brought his viewing site into the path of the oncoming stream of meteors until he was able to count more than 80 "falling stars" in a single hour. As the early morning light began to seep across the sky, he stumbled into the house, exhausted but elated. His dreams were filled with images of glowing objects sailing silently across a pitch black universe in a busy patchwork of stars and airplanes and meteors and planets and satellites.

His nightly ritual, now enhanced by the addition of cigar and martini, continued for the next two weeks until Vera confronted him one evening as he was about to step out onto the deck.

"Henry," she announced in a firm voice, "tomorrow night we are having dinner with Mr. and Mrs. Wendemere."

Henry didn't reply but raised his eyebrows questioningly.

"She is head of the women's group of the symphony," Vera explained, "and her husband is president of the local electric utility. They are very influential in this community, and I think it's time we got to know them."

Henry shrugged. "Okay," he said.

"And besides," she went on, "these new habits of yours are beginning to worry me — sitting out there all night, every night, and now you're smoking and drinking — I don't know what's come over you. Maybe if we go out more often it will be good for you."

"Okay," Henry repeated. Then, with a cigar in one hand and a cocktail glass in the other, clutching his martini pitcher under his arm, he pushed through the door and went out onto the deck, letting the door slam shut behind him. Vera looked after him for a long time before she finally turned and left the kitchen.

The next night they arrived at the Wendemeres' large brick home, and George Wendemere welcomed Henry with a firm handshake as Mrs. Wendemere ushered everyone into the living room.

"Would anyone like a drink?" Mr. Wendemere boomed. He was a short but athletic-looking man with a ruddy complexion and an easy smile. Henry found himself warming to his new acquaintance.

"A martini would be nice," Henry ventured.

Wendemere raised his index finger and pointed it at Henry. "I believe you're right on the mark!" he exclaimed. He turned to Vera. "Shall I make it two?"

"No thank you; nothing for me," Vera demurred.

Mrs. Wendemere also declined, and as she showed them to their seats and George headed for the bar, Vera shot Henry a withering glance, but he didn't appear to notice.

The dinner went by pleasantly enough and then the couples moved into a cozy den where Mrs. Wendemere poured coffee for herself and Vera, and George poured glasses of port for himself and Henry. After several minutes of small talk with various subjects trotted out and dying for lack of a second, Henry turned to George and asked, "Have you ever looked at the sky at night? I mean *really looked* closely?"

"Well, no, certainly not recently," George admitted.

"Oh, you really should," Henry said. "It's fascinating. You wouldn't believe how much activity there is up there — not just the manmade things, the planes and satellites, but the planets and moons and meteors — it's just incredible!"

As Henry went on, the passion that had been building in him the past several months spilled out as he described in great detail the four largest moons of Jupiter, which were first seen by Galileo in the 17th century. "They just look like pinpoints of white light along a straight line on both sides of Jupiter, and as they orbit the planet, the moons change position from one night to the next, like beads sliding along a wire," he gushed. "The discovery of these moons was a really big thing at the time because it was the first evidence that any other planet besides Earth had even one moon, let alone several."

Henry explained that Antares means "rival of Mars" because that bright orange star appears in the southwest near Mars and "outshines" the red planet at certain times of the year, and he told them how Mercury sometimes disappears in the solar glare and how Venus sometimes outshines everything but the moon. And he described the excitement of the meteor storms — the Perseid, the Leonid, and the Geminid — and how the full moon that occurs nearest the September equinox is called the Harvest Moon because its bright light enables farmers to continue working in the fields at night to bring in the fall crops.

As he spoke his eyes sparkled, and his hands traced patterns in the air, attempting to paint for his companions a picture of the wonders he had seen.

In the car on the way home, Vera was seething. After a long, icy silence, she said, "Well, I expect that's the last we'll see of the Wendemeres."

"Oh?" Henry responded. "He seemed like a nice fellow. I like him."

"They're wonderful people!" Vera snapped, turning toward him. "And they certainly didn't deserve to be tortured by you going on and on and on about the stupid stars!"

Henry frowned. "George seemed to be interested in what I was saying."

"That's because he's polite," Vera said. "*Nobody's* interested in all that except you because it's *boring.*

Now they're going to think that my husband's a crack-pot, and word will get around, and we'll never be invited anywhere!"

"Well, I'm sorry you feel that way," Henry said. "I thought it was a nice evening. I enjoyed it."

They rode the rest of the way home in silence.

The next afternoon Henry was even more restless than usual as he waited for the sun to drop behind the hills. The discussion the night before had left him filled with renewed enthusiasm for his hobby, and he couldn't wait to get back to his telescope. After wandering idly through the house (trying to avoid any further confrontations with Vera), he made his way back to the kitchen, looked at his watch, and growled, "The heck with it!" Then he mixed up a pitcher of martinis and headed for the deck. It was two o'clock in the afternoon.

He sat back in his chair and tried to relax, lighting a cigar with a big wooden kitchen match and watching the smoke he expelled roll away in clouds and then settle into layers in the still air. It was September, and the foliage on certain species of trees and shrubs was beginning to change color. He still knew some of them from his childhood — the red of sassafras, the yellow of hickory, and the bright orange of maple. From the house, the surrounding landscape fell away in a series of rolling hills, ending in a large, flat meadow. Beyond that meadow, still green, another series of hills rose, leading up to a high ridge perhaps half a mile away.

On that ridge stood the only signs of encroaching civilization — a cluster of apartment buildings that had been under construction throughout the spring and summer and now appeared complete.

On impulse, Henry swung the telescope around and pointed it at the distant buildings. He peered into the eyepiece and twisted the focusing knob, but all he could see was a green blur. He backed off on the magnification a couple of notches and again adjusted the focus. Now the green swatch was clear, and he could see its texture, but he still couldn't tell what it was. Again he clicked to a lower power, and now he could see what appeared to be a triangle of green cloth, tightly stretched, filled by an object that seem vaguely familiar.

Suddenly Henry jerked back from the telescope and his face turned very red. "It's a breast!" he thought, looking back at the door quickly to be sure Vera wasn't watching him. Taking a deep breath, he gradually regained his composure and slowly bent over the eyepiece. Yes, that's what it was — a female breast, barely contained by a small piece of green cloth. Henry noticed that his hands were trembling as he again decreased the magnification, revealing a woman in a bright green bikini. She was reclining on a chaise lounge, basking in the afternoon sun. As more details began to register, Henry realized she was a striking woman with a trim figure, finely shaped facial features, and waves of chestnut hair. She wore sunglasses, so he couldn't see her eyes, but he'd bet they were green. Henry thought she looked like Ann-Margret in that grumpy old guys movie with Lemmon and Matthau. She was that attractive.

"Henry!"

As Vera's voice crackled through the screen door, Henry jerked away from the telescope and knocked his martini glass off the table into a nearby flower pot, breaking the stem off the glass. He hastily swung the telescope around and nearly tripped over one leg of the tripod as he hurried toward the door, blushing furiously. He peered into the kitchen.

"What?" he asked, more brusquely than he intended, but if Vera noticed, she gave no indication.

"I just wondered what you'd like for dinner," Vera said. "I thought maybe you'd like to grill those salmon steaks I bought."

Turning back toward the deck, Henry waved his hand behind his head, in dismissal. "Yeah, sure, that's fine. I'll grill'em. Let me know when you're ready."

He picked up the bowl and stem of his martini glass and stared forlornly at the pieces. His cigar had rolled off the edge of the patio table and now lay cold upon the deck. After a moment, he carefully placed the broken glass on the table and moved quietly back to the door. Inside he could see Vera, standing with her back to him, chopping vegetables at the kitchen sink. He moved back to the telescope and pointed it again toward the apartments. He tried to keep his hands steady as he searched again for the same location and carefully adjusted the focusing knob. But he found only an empty chair. She was gone.

The next morning, Vera complained of a migraine and asked Henry to do the grocery shopping. With list in hand, he roamed the aisles of the supermarket until he finally located all of the items and, with a full cart, took his place in line at one of the checkout stations. He was going over his list one last time to be sure he had checked off everything when a voice behind him said, "Excuse me. Do you mind if I go ahead? I only have three items."

Henry turned and found himself face to face with the woman from the apartment. She was even more beautiful than he had thought, and — yes — her eyes were green. Henry blushed furiously, tried to move his cart out of her way, and stammered, "Oh, yes, of course. Please go ahead. I'm in no hurry."

"Thank you," she smiled, and then, much to Henry's surprise, she extended her hand and said, "I'm Roxanne Weatherby. I live in those new condos just outside of town."

As he took her firm, warm hand in his, Henry's mind raced, and he managed to stop himself from blurting out, "Yes, I know." Instead he mumbled his name and added, "It's very nice to meet you."

Then she moved on up the line, paid for her purchases, and was gone. But her perfume and the touch of her hand lingered. Henry felt as if he were in a daze as he loaded the grocery bags in the car and headed home. His life had taken an unexpected twist that left him utterly confused. Disconnected thoughts were flying through his mind like film through a runaway projector. But as he drove along the familiar road a degree of calmness returned, and by the time he reached the house he thought, "Maybe I just need a martini."

Henry went to the supermarket at exactly the same time every day for the next five days, but Roxanne (as he thought of her now) did not appear. He made no attempt to understand or explain his actions; he had no plan in mind, and no expectations. He had no sexual fantasies about her; he simply wanted to see her again, and on the sixth day he did.

He was browsing through the magazine section when he caught a glimpse of her flowing auburn hair as she breezed into the store and turned down an aisle toward the produce department. From a distance, he watched as she picked her way through the fresh fruits and vegetables, stopping here and there to squeeze this one or sniff that one and occasionally place a selection in her basket.

As she started toward the checkout lines, Henry set himself on a collision course and, when he was a few feet away from her, began waving and called, "Hi, there!"

She stopped and turned, looking at him with a quizzical expression.

"It's Roxanne, isn't it?" Henry asked as he grew nearer. "We met here last week, I believe. I'm Henry."

Remembering, she smiled, and Henry's heart began to pound. He felt he was jabbering insanely, but he couldn't stop himself.

"I live out on Curry's Pike just north of those condominiums," he blurted. "So we're practically neighbors."

Desperately he searched his mind for words — any words — to fill the void, to hold her here, even for a few more seconds.

"Listen," he heard himself say, "would you be offended if I offered to buy you a cup of coffee next door? I mean, since we're neighbors and everything. People don't get to know their neighbors anymore, and I think it's a shame."

She looked deep into his eyes for a moment, and then the smile returned. "Sure," she said, glancing at her watch. "I have a little time right now. Just let me pay for these vegetables, and I'll meet you outside."

They found a table in the coffee shop next door and placed their orders. While they waited they engaged in small talk — how long they had lived in the area, their work, where they were from originally. But after the waiter brought their coffee, there was a lull in the conversation, and Henry grew tense. Again he searched his mind for something he could say to hold her attention.

"Tell me," he began, finally, "Have you ever looked at the night sky? I mean, *really looked*?"

Driving home, Henry scolded himself for going on and on about the stars and the planets and the meteors, but Roxanne had seemed genuinely interested. Then again, he had thought George Wendemere was interested, but Vera claimed George was merely being polite to hide his boredom. Maybe Roxanne, too, was just humoring him. Thinking of Vera, he realized he felt a little guilty about his meeting with Roxanne, even though he had done nothing improper. He was just being friendly, just having a cup of coffee with one of their neighbors. How could that be wrong?

Still, Henry's mind was all a'flutter, with thoughts and ideas and images rushing off in all directions. He couldn't seem to pin down any one of those thoughts long enough to examine it. He felt as if time were speeding up, as if he were rushing toward something he couldn't yet see or understand.

Just as he reached the turnoff to his house, Henry stopped, turned the vehicle around and drove across the valley to the ridge. He drove slowly past Roxanne's condo but saw no sign of her. As he continued up the road looking for a place to turn around he came upon an eerie sight.

Along the south side of the road were enormous blocks of limestone in huge, jumbled piles like enormous gray dice thrown by some careless giant. They covered the entire hillside, some piles taller than a two-story building, many partially covered with vines, weeds, and even small trees struggling to take root.

Henry continued to drive slowly, taking in the spectacular otherwordly landscape, until he came to a large gate with a dilapidated sign: *Hoosier Limestone Company. Absolutely NO TRESPASSING!*

A few feet away, a section of the fence was unhooked and curled back from its metal post, creating a significant opening. A path cutting through the weeds beyond the opening indicated considerable foot traffic.

"Apparently a lot of people ignore the sign," Henry thought.

He parked the car and followed the path through the fence and its winding route through the underbrush until he found himself at the edge of a high cliff overlooking a body of water.

"An abandoned quarry," he thought. In an open area along the top of the precipice someone had left the remains of a campfire, and far below an inflatable raft was tied to a tree branch at the edge of the water.

Henry stood at the edge for a long time, looking down into the impenetrable depths of the water which, from this angle, appeared as black as night. He remembered hearing a story when he was a boy about a train locomotive that plunged into a water-filled quarry, into such a bottomless pit that it was never recovered. He shivered suddenly, turned and headed back to the car.

That night he had two martinis before dinner, and after the meal was finished he was mixing up a pitcher to take onto the deck when Vera asked him to step into the living room.

"I need to talk to you," she said.

Vera sat on the sofa, staring at her hands, which were folded on her knees. Henry remained standing.

"I'm not happy here, Henry," she began. "I want us to sell this place and move back to the city. There's no life here for me, and it's been even worse since you began acting so strangely. I'm truly concerned that you're having some sort of mental breakdown."

"But Vera —" Henry began, but she cut him off.

"I'm not going to debate this with you, Henry," she went on. "If you won't leave this place I'm going without you. I've already spoken to an attorney, and he explained that I *do* have some say-so in this." A tear slid down her cheek. "I have a right to be happy, too," she whispered.

Henry looked at her for a long moment. "You're right, Vera," he said finally. "I haven't paid much attention to your feelings. I'm sorry."

After another lengthy pause, Henry quietly left the room.

That night, as he sat out on his deck, scanning the sky with his telescope, his cigar seemed flavorless, and the icy martinis brought him no comfort. Even the sight of brilliant white Jupiter rising in the east failed to excite him. Yellow Saturn followed about forty minutes later, trailing Jupiter across the sky, but Henry barely looked at the two planets.

Then, just before midnight, Henry became aware of a distant object that seemed to be moving slowly but steadily in his direction. He brought the telescope to bear, but the object appeared only as a glowing sphere; he could not make out any details. Slowly but relentlessly it continued its approach, growing larger and larger. Henry put aside the telescope and stood, his eyes fixed on the strange white orb as it continued toward him, still increasing in size. He could see now that it was huge — as wide as a football field and taller than a house. It made no sound but seemed to pulsate with light from within. Its creamy white, smooth exterior showed no seams and no openings of any kind and appeared almost translucent, like fine porcelain. Henry stood transfixed as the object paused above him. He felt only awe as he struggled to understand what he was seeing.

"I'm not!" Henry blurted suddenly, and then he realized he was responding to an admonition: "Do not be afraid," although he had not actually heard those words. There had been no sound.

"We mean you no harm."

Again, no words had been spoken, and yet the message was clear.

"We are here to learn and to share our knowledge with you."

Henry stood agape, eager for the next byte of information.

"Our mission is ongoing and includes many cultures, many civilizations."

Henry's pulse pounded. He had never felt such excitement.

"Would you like to come with us?"

Henry stood staring up at the magnificent object, its glow reflecting off his face, and he slowly raised his arms as if to embrace it.

"Oh, yes!" he whispered.

"Is there one you wish to accompany you?"

Henry thought immediately of Vera and their life together. It saddened him to think how unhappy she had been after being plucked from the life she had known in the city.

Then he turned and looked down to the moonlit meadow below, to the hills beyond and the distant ridge on the opposite side of the valley. And he smiled.

One week later Vera opened the front door to find Detective Blake and one of his fellow officers.

"I'm sorry to bother you again, ma'am, but we have some new leads concerning your husband's disappearance," the detective said.

Vera showed the officers into the living room.

"I was wondering if you know a woman by the name of Roxanne Weatherby," the detective continued.

Vera shook her head. "No. I've never heard the name."

"Well, I hate to have to tell you this, but we believe

your husband knew her," Blake said. "We think they were having an affair."

Vera's hand flew to her face. "Oh!" she gasped.

"They were seen together at a coffee shop in town, and it turns out she disappeared the same night your husband vanished," Blake continued.

Vera sat down on the couch. Her face was very pale. "This is all such a shock," she said softly.

The detective pulled up a chair and sat facing her. He held a small notebook in his left hand and tapped it nervously with his right index finger.

"The strange thing is, this woman took nothing with her. Her clothes, her makeup, her purse, car keys, credit cards — they were all still in her apartment, her car still in its parking space. Do you know if your husband might have had a large amount of cash with him?"

Again Vera shook her head. "No. I checked with the bank like you said, and they told me all the accounts are fine; there haven't been any unusual withdrawals."

"Did your husband have any credit cards with him?"

"He had two, as far as I know," Vera answered. "One for routine purchases and one we used only for emergencies. Henry doesn't believe in running up a lot of credit card debt."

Detective Blake stood. "We'll need those card numbers," he said. "They're our best hope of finding your husband. Sooner or later he'll use one of them, and when he does we'll know exactly where he and this woman are."

But no one ever used the credit cards, and the authorities never found Henry, and they never found Roxanne. And they never found an explanation for the huge ring of charred vegetation that appeared in the lower meadow the night the two of them vanished from the earth.

No Redemption

Take therefore no thought for the morrow . . .
Sufficient unto the day is the evil thereof."
— *Matthew 6:34*

J ust a few miles outside the small village of Leota,
light was fading quickly as the sun dropped behind
the western hills. A cold wind was spitting snow.

Two men on horseback turned off the main road
and approached a farmstead. The frozen, rutted lane
was barely visible through the remnants of an earlier
snowfall. The riders passed by a large barn and pulled
up in front of the neat clapboard-sided home. Kerosene
lamps glowed warmly in the curtained windows.

The older man stepped down from his horse and
paused to take in his surroundings. He was not a tall
man but, although his hair was graying, he conveyed
an impression of physical strength. On his right hip he

wore a Colt revolver with well-worn walnut grips and on his left a heavy Bowie knife in a leather sheath, the handle facing forward. His winter coat was sheepskin, and he wore brown leather gloves.

"I'll do the talking," he said as he shook the snow from his wide-brimmed hat and moved toward the porch.

The younger man was whippet thin with sharp features and dark eyes that darted nervously here and there as he swung down from his horse. A limp hank of coal black hair hung across his forehead. He was dressed all in black — trousers, boots, shirt, vest and hat — and he wore a fancy black tooled-leather gun belt with a bone-handled .45 in the holster, tied down with a leather thong. He wore a gray wool overcoat and black wool gloves.

Inside the house, a middle-aged farmer in bib overalls sat at the kitchen table finishing a cup of coffee while his wife cleared away the supper dishes. A young girl sat in a chair, sewing, and across the room a boy was sprawled in front of the fireplace, reading a book.

When the knock came at the door, the farmer glanced around at the others, said, "Wonder who that could be?" and rose to answer.

As the door opened the older of the two riders swept off his hat. "Evenin', sir," he said. "My friend and I were hopin' you might be able to spare a bite to eat for a couple of cold and weary travelers."

"I'm afraid you've missed supper," the farmer answered hesitantly as he studied the visitors.

"My name is Gordon Cole," the man offered, "and this is Charlie Sneed," gesturing with his hat toward the thin man.

"But folks just call me Snake!" the slender man blurted, grinning. The comment drew a disapproving frown from his companion.

"We have work waiting for us up at Rockford," Cole told the farmer. "But apparently we misjudged how long it would take us to get there on horseback."

The farmer studied the two men for a few more seconds and then stepped back and opened the door.

"Well, we can offer you some coffee, and there might be some cornbread left," he said.

"We'd be much obliged," Cole replied. As they stepped through the door, he nudged Sneed and indicated with a toss of his head that he also should remove his hat.

The two men sat at the kitchen table and wolfed down cornbread and butter and drank the strong, hot coffee the farmer's wife brought them. The farmer sat back in his chair, observing them thoughtfully.

"You men cross the river at Utica?" he asked.

"We did," Cole said, "on the ferry."

"You know, it's going to be at least a week yet before you get to Rockford on horseback. Would'a been a lot quicker to take the train."

Cole finished off a final bite of cornbread and washed it down with coffee before looking up from his plate.

"I'm sure that's true," he said. "Unfortunately we don't have sufficient funds to make the trip by train. But we do have a couple of good horses."

"What kind of work do you fellas do?" the farmer asked.

The man called Snake started to speak, but Cole cut him off.

With a dismissive gesture, he said, "Oh, logging . . . sawmill labor . . . a little carpentry — whatever we can find." He shifted in his chair and looked around the room. "Appears to me you've done right well with your farm here. Sturdy barns, a frame house instead of a cabin, comfortable furnishings — what's your cash crop?"

The farmer frowned, uncomfortable with the inquiry.

"We don't deal in cash much around here," he said. "I raise corn to feed my hogs and cattle, and we butcher in the fall. My wife and the children tend a large garden and put up vegetables for the winter. We have chickens for eggs and meat. Not much need for cash money."

Before Cole could stop him Snake chortled, "Still and all, I bet you got a nice little nest egg put back somewheres safe — under the mattress, maybe?"

"Mr. Sneed," Cole said firmly, "it's not polite to inquire about such things." He turned back to the farmer. "I apologize for my untutored friend, Mr. — Oh my, here we've been enjoying your hospitality and I didn't even get your name!"

"It's Hostettler," the farmer said. "Oren Hostettler."

The farmer rose from his chair as if preparing to show the men out. They also pushed back their chairs and stood.

"So you're both assured of work once you get to Rockford?" Hostettler asked.

"Oh yes," Cole said. "We got a letter last Tuesday from Mr. Harlan Rieckers who runs the big timber operation and sawmill up there, encouraging us to come and join his crew."

The farmer frowned. "This letter was from Mr. Rieckers himself?"

"Yep," Cole said, "and we were mighty glad to get it."

"Well, that's confusing," Hostettler said, scratching his head. "I heard Harlan Rieckers was killed back in November when a chain broke and a pile of logs rolled onto him."

There was a frozen smile on Cole's face. "Well, you know how slow the mail is these days," he said.

He stepped forward as if to thank the farmer for his hospitality but suddenly raised his left hand and gripped the farmer's shoulder. In the same instant the big Bowie knife appeared in Cole's right hand, and he drove the blade to the hilt beneath Hostettler's breastbone, then shoved even harder as if trying to force it up into his heart.

The two men stood still for a few seconds. Cole's left hand still gripped the farmer's shoulder while his right continued to keep pressure on the knife. He stared into the farmer's eyes as Hostettler began to sag against the table.

The wife, seeing him fall, screamed. The boy dropped the book he had been reading and leapt across the room, reaching up for an old rifle that hung on pegs on the wall.

A gunshot roared, and the boy, struck in the back by a .45 slug, slipped down, his outstretched fingers clawing at the wall until he hit the floor and lay still.

"Whooee!" Snake yelled in a high-pitched, nervous voice. "One pigstuck and one backshot! Whooee, boys!" For a moment it seemed as if he would break into a jig. Smoke was still curling from the barrel of his pistol.

By this time the woman was kneeling over the body of her husband, sobbing. Cole stood watching her and wiping the knife blade with a kitchen towel.

Then Snake noticed the girl, cowering in a corner, whimpering, clutching the garment she had been sewing. He seized her by her golden curls and pulled her to him.

"Hey, little girl," he cackled, "c'mere and see what old Snake's got for you!"

Cole crossed the room in two long strides and slapped his partner across the face. Snake jumped back with a snarl, crouching. His right hand touched the grip of his pistol. But he didn't draw. "What'd you go and do that for?" he whined.

"Shit-for-brains!" Cole spat. "Those old boys up at

Rockford will bid a fancy price to have first go at that little girl. I let you have your way with her, we'll be lucky to get six bits!"

As Cole's reasoning sunk in, Snake began to calm down. Then Cole added, "Do what you want with the woman," and Snake laughed. He grabbed the woman by the arm and dragged her away from her husband's body and into an adjoining room. For a while her screams filled the house but then stopped abruptly.

Cole ransacked the rest of the house and found a small box of cash under some clothes in a dresser drawer.

Later, after the two men got the girl mounted between them on the farmer's good saddle horse, the trio rode off into the night. Behind them, fire flickered through the windows of the farmhouse. Soon the blaze consumed the entire structure, which finally collapsed in on itself in an explosion of flame, smoke, and swirling embers that spiraled high into the night sky as the killers rode away.

The bar, which was located inside the hotel, smelled of stale beer, whiskey, and cigar smoke. In the late afternoon stillness of a January day, there were only two customers, seated at separate tables, each lost in his own thoughts. The bartender, a large, fair-skinned man with a thick shock of white hair, busied himself by polishing shot glasses with a corner of his long, white apron.

All eyes turned as the front door swung open and a man stepped inside, accompanied by swirling snow and howling wind. He turned and shut the door and then stood for a moment, surveying the room and allowing his eyes to adjust to the gloom as he removed his black leather gloves. His height was accentuated by stove-pipe boots, a long, military style overcoat of gray wool, and a wide-brimmed black hat. His stern gaze quickly assessed the salesman who was sipping whiskey at a table in the corner and the skinner drinking beer at a table closer to the bar. Then his eyes brightened and a smile broke through his salt-and-pepper beard as he strode across the room to the bartender and extended his hand.

"Swede! It's good to see you," he said, warmly. "How are you?"

"Oh, I do okay, Sam. Can't complain," the bartender replied, shaking the man's hand. "How 'bout you? You got official business here?"

"No." He shook his head. "I'm just passing through, heading south. May be my last trip — I'm going to be retiring in a couple of weeks."

"Well, that is news!" the bartender said. "This calls for a drink — on the house!" He placed a glass on the bar and poured a shot of whisky.

The man raised the glass, nodded, and tossed back the drink. "Thanks, Swede." He rested a boot on the bar's brass rail and settled in, removing his hat and placing it on the bar. "Well, since Sarah and I got married last year, I've been thinking a lot about hanging up my guns and giving up the badge. We're going to make our home on her farm, start a whole new chapter while I've still got time. I'd like to plant some apple trees; I always thought I'd like to have an orchard."

"It will seem strange not having you be the marshal no more," Swede said. "You been riding herd on this district for a long time."

"Too long," the man agreed. "After so many years it begins to wear on a fellow — all the ways people find to do bad things to each other. There's just no end to it." He shrugged. "Well, anyway . . . how about another whisky? On me this time."

At that, the skinner at the nearby table stirred to life. He was a heavy, red-faced, bloated man, clad in a suit of greasy buckskin. A matted tangle of long hair hung almost to his shoulders. His wide belt supported both a heavy army pistol and a long-bladed knife. He struggled to his feet and moved unsteadily toward the bar.

"Say," he growled. "Sounds like some kind of celebration's going on here. Maybe somebody would offer to buy a man a drink." He stood by the bar, weaving slightly, his glassy eyes fixed on the man called Sam.

"Hey, you should know who you're addressin' here," the bartender said. "You happen to be talking to Samuel S. Stone, U.S. district marshal."

The skinner blinked, belched, and then squinted as if trying to see the marshal more clearly. "Well, like I said," he persisted, "seems to me somebody might buy a man a drink."

Stone regarded the man for a moment and then smiled. "What'll you have?"

The skinner drew himself up to the bar. "Well, whisky then," he mumbled. He received his drink and sipped it slowly as the bartender and Stone continued their conversation. As they talked, the man stared down into the glass and frowned fiercely as if struggling to focus on some far away object. Then he turned and fixed the same intense gaze on Stone.

"Some years back there was a lawman down at Madison," he mumbled, finally.

Stone and the bartender continued their conversation, unaware the man was speaking to them.

"He brought in Tommy Clampitt to go on trial for killin' some storekeeper and his wife," the skinner went on. "Do you remember that?"

"What?" Stone turned to the man. "I'm sorry. Did you say something?"

"Tommy Clampitt," the skinner repeated. "Do you know that name?"

"No, not that I recall," Stone said. "Who is he?"

The skinner leaned closer. "He's — he was — my nephew; my own brother's son. Five, six years ago, they said he killed a storekeeper and his wife down at Madison. There was a big trial. He was just a kid . . ."

"Ah," Stone said. "Yes. I remember the case. I didn't remember the name."

The skinner rambled on, becoming more and more agitated. "I was out in Missouri when it happened; didn't hear about it till I got back, and then it was too late. He was just a kid and they hung him for murder." As he talked, the skinner's hand began to inch toward his pistol.

"I do remember something about the case," Stone said. "As I recall, they had the mistaken idea there was a large amount of cash hidden in the store. They tortured the man and then raped his wife in front of him, trying to make him talk. When they finally ran out of patience, the young fellow shot the storekeeper in the face at point-blank range, and when the woman tried to come to her husband's aid, he crushed her skull with the barrel of his pistol. All for eight dollars and a bottle of whisky."

The skinner didn't seem to hear but continued to mumble. "He was just a kid . . . my brother's son, my very own nephew — he was family. And they killed him without no more care than a rabbit. That judge said he had to hang, and, by god, the marshal took him out and hung him." His eyes widened as if he had just begun to understand his own words. "*You* were that marshal," he blurted. "You're the one hung my nephew!"

Stone's eyes grew cold. "He needed hanging," he said.

The skinner's hand closed around the grips of his pistol, and he started to slide the weapon from its holster. His face was dark with drunken fury, his eyes blazing with reckless hatred.

Just as the man's gun cleared leather, Stone reached across the bar in a single smooth motion, grasped the neck of the whisky bottle and brought it around in a whistling arc to smash across the skinner's forehead. The heavy bottle shattered, and the skinner was thrown back from the bar, crashing onto a table and overturning it. He hit the floor on his back, lay there for a moment, and then slowly tried to pull himself up, grasping the overturned table for support. The whisky bottle had opened a gash across his forehead, and blood was streaming down his face, mingling with the remains of the liquor. His eyes were open wide in a glazed stare. He managed to get to his feet, took one halting step forward and then collapsed face down and lay still.

Stone sighed and picked up his hat. He looked down at the unconscious man and shook his head. "It's getting so a man can't even have a drink in peace," he said. "See you, Swede." He flipped some coins onto the bar and headed back out into the winter storm.

As his horse picked its way along the trail, Stone could barely see the blue outline of a range of hills in the distance through the steadily falling snow. As he approached the base of the first ridge, the open flat land gave way to a mix of cedar and pine trees and assorted hardwoods that loomed darkly as the trail began to climb.

As he rode he thought about Sarah and how her presence had changed his life. Stone had lived on his own for more than forty years after his first wife was killed in a tragic incident. He blamed himself for her death.

He had been wearing a town marshal's badge for only a couple of years, and he and Mary had been married for only a short time.

It started like any ordinary day. He was walking toward the courthouse when he saw Mary across the street, in front of the bank. She waved to him, and he started to cross to her when all hell broke loose.

A hard case by the name of Dillon Clegg burst through the front door of the bank. He and his men were robbing the place. When Clegg saw Stone, he grabbed Mary and pulled her in front of him as a shield. He had one arm around her waist, and his other hand held a pistol to her head. He didn't say anything but just held her like that as he shuffled sideways toward the hitching post and his horse.

Stone was young and full of piss and vinegar, and he didn't hesitate. In one smooth motion, he brought up his .44, took aim at Clegg, and pulled the trigger.

Just as he fired, Clegg made a break for it. He shoved Mary away from him, toward Stone, and the marshal's bullet struck her in the head. She was dead before he reached her side. By then the county sheriff had heard the commotion and came running from the courthouse. Just as Clegg started to ride off down the street the sheriff shot him out of the saddle — dead.

Stone knew if he had waited just one more second,

Mary would still be alive. And Clegg would have met his end just as he did. He had struggled with that guilt for all these years. But Sarah had helped him come to terms with it.

When he had come to know her and told her his story, she placed her hand on his. "Oh, Sam," she said, "you had no way to know it would turn out like that. You had to make a split-second decision, and you tried to save your wife. You're a good man, and you have to put the blame where it belongs — on the outlaw Clegg. His actions brought all that about. You can't take it all on yourself. You have to let it go. If you don't, it will turn in on you, and destroy all the good in you."

Stone had felt her slender fingers squeezing his hand.

"I think it may be too late," he said. "When I was first appointed marshal, I had the idealism of youth. But as time went on, I began to realize that I was tracking down many of the same criminals time after time, and each year brought more just like them. Sometimes I think I've become more like the men I hunt than the man I used to be."

He shook his head and added, "I know what they say: 'Marshal Stone takes no prisoners.' I'm not proud of that reputation."

"But we need men like you, Sam. We need strong men who will make the hard decisions for us and do what's necessary to protect us. Without you and others like you, this would be a savage wilderness where no one but thieves and killers could survive. You have to stop being so hard on yourself."

He smiled, but the smile didn't erase the sadness in his eyes. He squeezed her hand. "You're a kind and wise woman, Sarah," he said. "Morgan was a lucky man."

Stone and Sarah's first husband, Morgan, had ridden together during the war, and in the years after, Stone had occasionally visited them at their farm. But three years earlier, Morgan had suffered a stroke and was gone within a week. The marshal only learned of his friend's death when he stopped by the farm a month later.

After Morgan died, his brother, Charles, and his wife bought the farm next to Sarah's. Charles took care of the farming, and his wife and Sarah worked together doing the gardening, putting up fruits and vegetables for the winter, taking care of the laundry and mending — all the household chores. And Sarah helped look after their children.

Stone would stop by and visit with them when he was passing through, and over time he began to realize he was attracted to Sarah. But his guilt about Mary's death and his friendship with Morgan made it difficult for him to admit his feelings.

Then one evening when they were sitting by the fireplace talking, Sarah revealed her fondness for him.

"Morgan was a good man," she said, "just as you are, Sam. But he's gone, and your Mary's gone, and the past is gone. But we're still here, and we still have a future, and a chance for some happiness."

She stood and pulled him to his feet. She drew close and kissed him.

"We still have a life to live, Sam," she said, "I've grown to care for you these last few years, and I think you could care for me if you'd just let go of the past. There's still time for us to have a good life together."

He brought her into his arms and kissed her deeply. Then, placing his hands on her shoulders, he looked into her eyes. "I never allowed myself to think you could feel that way about a man like me. But I've known for some time that I love you." He kissed her again.

After a moment, without another word, she took him by the hand and led him to her bed. They were married a month later.

As the last glow of daylight vanished behind the hills, Stone rode down into an open valley and saw the lights of their cabin. The smell of wood smoke reached him as he approached the house. A dog began barking, and the door opened just a crack. Sarah called out, "Who's there? Charles, is that you?"

The door swung open, and she peered into the gathering darkness. "Sam?" she asked, and then, seeing his face, she threw her arms around him and pulled him inside. "Oh, Sam! It is you. Come in and let me get you something to eat; you must be freezing!"

She fastened the door, took his hat and overcoat and hung them on a nearby peg, and then ushered him toward the kitchen table. "You just sit and warm yourself," she ordered. She went to the cast iron cook stove and poured a steaming mug of coffee from a blue granite pot. She set the mug in front of him. "Let me get you something to eat," she continued.

She hurried about the kitchen, serving him a bowl of hot stew, freshly baked bread, and more rich, dark coffee.

After the meal, Stone pulled a long, thin cigar from his inside pocket and lit it with a flaming twig from the fireplace. He exhaled a cloud of cigar smoke and watched it drift across the room toward the fireplace, where it disappeared up the chimney.

Sarah came from the kitchen and stood behind him, placing her hands on his shoulders. She leaned forward and kissed the top of his head.

"You can't imagine how I miss you when you're not here," she said. "I'll be so happy when you can come home to stay."

He reached up and took her hand.

"It won't be long now," he said.

The next morning, Stone was having his coffee when County Sheriff Arthur Killion came knocking at the door.

"Something real bad has happened out at the Hostettler farm," the sheriff said by way of greeting. He came inside and stood by the door holding his hat.

"Want some coffee?" the marshal asked.

"Naw," Killion said. "This is real bad. You need to go out there with me."

"All right," Stone replied. "But what's happened?"

The sheriff, who was twenty years the marshal's junior, twisted his hat in his hands. He told Stone what he knew about the slaughter of the Hostettler family.

Stone explained the situation to Sarah, and soon he and Killion were riding across the valley on their way to the scene of the crime.

Stone could smell the acrid smoke long before they reached the smoldering ruins of the farmhouse. A couple of the sheriff's deputies were using long sticks to poke around in the charred rubble. A man in a long black coat and top hat stood next to a wagon in which blankets covered what Stone assumed were bodies of the victims.

"We've found the bodies of Mr. Hostettler, his wife, and their boy, Isaac, but the neighbors say they also had a daughter, Rosalie, about fourteen years old," the sheriff said. "We ain't found any sign of her."

"So you figure they took her," the marshal mused, turning to look around at the barns and other outbuildings.

Killion nodded. He took a stubby briar pipe from his vest pocket and lit it with a wooden match. "We reckon there were just two of them," he said. He pointed toward the barn. "Neighbors said Hostettler had a bay mare, but it's gone. They probably put the girl on her daddy's horse. With the snow, it's easy to see the three sets of tracks heading off to the north there."

"I expect they're headed for Rockford," Stone said.

"That's what we figured," Killion agreed. "It's the only town of any size in that direction, and from what I've heard it's become a true den of thieves in recent years — a real outlaws' hideaway."

"It does attract a lot of miscreants," Stone said. "Not much there but saloons, gambling dens, and whorehouses." He took out one of his slim cigars and lit it. "Well, I reckon I'd better head that way."

"It would be out of your way at first," the sheriff said, "but if you rode over to New Albany and took the train it would be faster in the long run. You'd get there before they do."

"Yeah, but what if it turns out that's not where they're headed after all? I could lose them if they turn off somewhere along the way. I need to stick with their trail."

"Well, no doubt they've long since crossed the county line," Killion said, "but you can deputize some of my men to go with you."

"Thanks, but they'd just slow me down," Stone said.

"But you could use some help. It won't be easy for one man to bring two killers back all that way on horseback."

He followed as Stone strode over to his horse and swung into the saddle. The marshal sat staring off to the north as if lost in thought.

Killion looked up at the marshal for a moment and then said quietly, "You don't intend to bring them back, do you?"

Without another word, the marshal tipped his hat, swung the horse around, and rode off between the farm buildings, headed north.

The marshal followed the trail throughout the day, passing by the occasional hardscrabble farmstead and winding through forested hills of hickory, beech, maple and various oaks, all bare skeletons in their winter dormancy, except for the young beeches that clung stubbornly to a few russet leaves. Although there were patches where the snow had blown away, enough remained for him to follow the tracks of the three riders.

As sundown approached, the trail left the forest and dropped into a valley where chimney smoke rose from a small cabin. A narrow creek that followed along the base of the hills was mostly frozen, and its icy surface reflected the red and orange glow of the setting sun. Stone approached the cabin, dismounted, and led his horse into the attached lean-to, where there was a watering trough and a rack of hay. Leaving the horse to feed, he went to the cabin door, opened it and called out, "Hello! Willie? It's Sam Stone!"

Willie Hawkins, a wiry little man with unruly white hair and a stubble of whiskers, came toward him, grinning widely, revealing several gaps where teeth were missing. He wore a stained long-sleeved undershirt and patched canvas trousers.

"Sam! Come in, come in!" he gushed. He grabbed the marshal's hand, placed his other hand on the marshal's shoulder, and ushered him into the one-room space. "Take off your coat, have a seat, and I'll get ye some coffee. It's good to see ye!"

"Well, I was headed north and saw your smoke," Stone replied. "Thought I'd stop by, see how you were doing." He removed his hat, gloves and overcoat and tossed them on the bed in the corner of the room. He took a seat on a wooden chair in front of the fireplace and warmed his hands.

Hawkins poured him a mug of coffee from a blackened pot simmering on the wood-fired cookstove. The marshal took a sip. "Whew!" he exclaimed. "That'll put hair on your chest!"

Hawkins grinned. "Well, if ye want coffee there ain't no use in pussyfootin' around about it." He moved behind a battered and scarred wooden table, picked up the stub of a fat cigar resting precariously on the corner, and stuck it in his mouth. Then he grabbed a well-worn meat cleaver and began chopping up the skinned carcass of a rabbit that lay in the center of the table.

"You'll stay for supper, won't ye?" he asked. "Fried rabbit with biscuits and gravy. Mighty good eatin'."

Stone noticed the little shower of cigar ash that floated down onto the meat each time Hawkins chopped or spoke.

"Well, we'll see," the marshal said. "I need to stay on the trail of these killers." He told Hawkins what had happened — how three members of a family had been slaughtered and a young girl kidnapped.

"What I don't understand is what could have possessed them to let those two killers into their home," Stone said. He lit one of his cigars and leaned back in his chair. "Unless the two men forced their way in at gunpoint — I suppose that's likely. But then again, some people are just too trusting, you know? They don't realize what kind of marauders are running around out there."

Hawkins finished cutting up the rabbit and started rolling the pieces in flour. "Yeah, it pays to be a little suspicious sometimes," he said. "Bein' a good Samaritan out here can get you killed." He put a couple of big scoops of lard into a cast-iron skillet and set it on the cookstove. "What you said about folks being too trusting puts me in mind of old Billy Cochran. You remember him?"

Stone shook his head.

"His sidekick was a guy named Junior Dalton. I think they were cousins or something. Anyway, Billy was kind of slow. Well, to tell the truth, he didn't have sense enough to pour piss out of a boot. He'd do about anything Junior told him to do, which wasn't always a good thing."

Hawkins started dropping the floured pieces of rabbit into the hot grease.

"One summer, Junior and Billy and a couple of other no-goods were livin' on a sandbar in the river just west of town. They'd do some fishin', and every two or three days they'd take a basket of catfish to the cafe in town and sell them to the owner. Then they'd take the money and buy some rotgut liquor and head back to the sandbar.

"One night, when Junior and Billy'd drunk about all the whisky they could stand, they got into a big argument. One of their cohorts who told me about it didn't remember what the fight was about, but they were goin' at it tooth and nail."

Hawkins paused to turn some of the rabbit pieces with a long-handled fork. Then he went on with his story:

"They were yellin' at each other and carryin' on, and all of a sudden Junior cries, 'Wait a minute!' and they just froze and stood there lookin' at each other. Then Junior says to Billy, 'Let me borrow your knife,' and Billy, being a trusting sort, hands over his knife. Well, quicker'n a snake, Junior reaches out and cuts Billy — not much more'n a scratch, really — but right across his gut!

"Billy was shocked, of course. He looked down at his belly, and he looked up at Junior, and he said, "Well, Junie . . . If I'd a'knowed ye wuz a'gonna cut me I wouldn't a'loaned ye my knife!'"

Hawkins slapped his knee and chortled, and the marshal chuckled.

"Of course," the old man continued, "after a day or two Billy forgot all about it, and he and Junior were back thick as thieves again, fishin' and drinkin' and Billy followin' Junior around like some kind of pet rooster. But I guess everybody's got to find their own place in this world."

The old man piled the crispy fried rabbit on a platter and set it on the table. He added some flour and milk to the grease in the skillet, added salt and a good amount of pepper and stirred the mixture vigorously until it thickened into a gravy. Then he opened the cookstove oven and took out a tin pan full of biscuits.

"Time to eat!" he told the marshal, and they pulled their chairs up to the table.

"You know, this is pretty tasty," Stone said after a few bites. "I don't notice the cigar ashes at all."

Hawkins laughed. "Well, after my Agnes died, it was either learn to cook a few things or starve," he said.

They ate in silence for a few minutes before Stone said, "That story of yours about Billy and Junior reminds me of something that happened years ago down in Scott County."

He stepped over to the cookstove and refilled his coffee mug. As he walked back to his chair he explained, "There was a man named Eli Benton — a big, strong fellow but not very bright. He was convicted of killing a man in a bar fight, and the judge sentenced him to hang. When the day came, the local sheriff and I walked Eli up the stairs to the gallows. He looked around at the noose and the trapdoor and the lever that made it all work, and he turned to the sheriff and said, "Are you sure this thing's safe?"

Both men laughed; then Hawkins's expression grew more serious. "I heard a rumor they're gettin' ready to put you out to pasture," he said.

"No, it's time," Stone said. "I'm ready to hang it up — I've been at it too long. Marshaling's a young man's game."

"Well, they'll have a hell of a time finding someone to take your place. You've become something of a legend around here."

"I'm not so sure about that," Stone scoffed, "but if it was true that would be another sign it's time to quit."

"You sound almost eager to get out," Hawkins noted.

"I'll tell you the truth, Willie, I've been giving a lot of thought lately to all the things that have happened over the years — all the things I've done and seen. Being a lawman you get hardened after a while. When I was younger I felt like I was able to give people the benefit of the doubt sometimes — I tried to be fair — but I just don't have the patience anymore. The last few years people have started saying I'd just as soon shoot a criminal as go to the trouble of bringing him back to stand trial. I don't think that was my intention starting out, but lately I'm starting to think they might be right."

Hawkins sat forward in his chair. "Aw, Sam, you have to defend yourself. Most of those fellas'd just as soon shoot ye as look at ye. Can't worry too much about tryin' to be fair to somebody who aims to kill you!"

The marshal puffed on his cigar and blew out a string of smoke rings. "Do you ever think back on your life, Willie, and wonder if you could have been a better person?"

"Oh, there's no doubt I could've been a better person. But I think I can say I never went out of my way to hurt anybody. I found a good woman, and Agnes and I raised two sons who have always worked hard and are taking care of their own families now, so I'm content. I figure that's about the best I ever could have hoped for. Besides, doesn't do any good to fret about what might have been, and you shouldn't either."

"I reckon," Stone said.

"You're a good man, Sam, and you should look forward to drawin' your pension and livin' in peace, not worryin' about the past. You've done a good job at what you were hired to do. Be content. That would be my advice, for whatever it's worth. Just be content."

Hawkins rose, crossed to a small cupboard, and drew out a bottle of whisky and two glasses. "Here," he said, "let's have a drink. I'll get you a blanket and you can curl up there in front of the fire and get some sleep. I doubt if those folks you're followin' will ride all night long. They have to rest too. You can catch up to them in the morning."

"Thanks, Willie," Stone said. "I appreciate it — the food, the whisky, and the chance to just shoot the breeze with somebody my own age. I miss that sometimes."

The marshal sipped the whisky and stared into the crackling fire. After a while he drifted off and dreamed he was riding across a vast open meadow without a cloud in the bright blue sky.

Cole and Snake, with the Hostettler girl between them, followed the northbound trail as it entered another hilly area of hardwood forest. Off to the left, among the trees, Cole spotted a squat, shed roof structure built of logs. There was a single window made of oiled paper, and there was smoke coming from the chimney.

Cole and Snake dismounted and tied the horses to a wobbly hitching post. Cole lifted the girl down from her mount and handed her off to Snake, who took her by the arm. Cole drew his revolver and moved quietly up to the door. He listened intently but heard no sounds from inside.

He opened the door and stepped inside, covering the room with his pistol. The only occupant was a very large black man dozing in a rocking chair in front of the fireplace.

"Uh-hem!" Cole cleared his throat, and the other man opened his eyes and spoke.

"Say, now! Can I do somethin' for you?"

Cole still had the gun in his hand, but now it was pointed casually at the floor. "We're traveling through, and we didn't know what kind of place this was. Thought maybe it was a way station where we could get some food and a room for the night."

"We can work somethin' out like that," the man said, rising from his chair. He looked around the single open room, waving an open palm as if pointing out its features.

"It ain't fancy, but it's warm and dry, and I'm cookin' up some beans with a ham hock that should be right tasty. Got cornbread, too."

Again, he pointed around the room. "There ain't no beds, but you can spread your bedrolls on the floor and spend the night out of the cold. It's a dirt floor, but it's packed down good, and I keep it swept. Ain't no rocks in it. A dollar a night from each of you for dinner and a place to sleep. Outhouse is out back. If you want a chamber pot that's twenty-five cents extra."

"Sounds fair," Cole said. He turned back toward the door, but the man added, "Payment in advance is customary."

Cole turned, gave him a hard look, and then shrugged. He counted out some coins from a small leather poke and handed it to the man. Then he crossed to the door, opened it, and motioned for Snake and the girl to come in.

"This here's my associate, Mr. Sneed," Cole said, "but we just call him Snake." He pointed to the girl. "And this is my niece, Rosalie. We're escorting her up to Rockford to meet up with some of the family."

"Pleased to meet you all," the black man said, touching his forehead as if tipping a hat. "I'm Lucius. Lucius Poppelwell."

He spread his hands and looked around the room again as if inviting them to do the same. "Make yourselfs at home. There's hot coffee on the cookstove, and we'll have beans and cornbread in two shakes of a lamb's tail. And you can warm yourselfs in front of the fire."

Snake strolled around the room, looking at the meager furnishings. Cole grabbed a graniteware cup from a sideboard and poured himself some coffee. He took one sip and spat it out. With a quick flick of his wrist he sent the rest of the contents flying halfway across the room, splattering on the floor.

"I don't know what this is, but it sure as hell ain't coffee!" he said.

Lucius, feeling embarrassed, said, "I make it myself — out of chicory and ground up dried acorns. I'm so used to it I don't even think about it no more."

Shaking his head, Cole barked: "Snake, go get that bag of coffee beans out of my saddlebag." He turned back to Lucius and said, "I ain't drinkin' this shit."

"That's fine, suh. If you got real coffee with you that would be a blessin'." He thought for a moment and added, "I wouldn't drink this shit either if real coffee wuzn't so dear."

When Snake returned, he handed the cloth bag to Cole. "I'll make us some real coffee," Cole said. "While I'm doin' that you'd better walk that girl to the outhouse and let her do her business. Bring her right back, and don't mess with her."

The girl rose and pulled her blanket tight around her. With her head down, she moved slowly toward the door.

"We ain't got all night," Snake said. He put his hand on her upper back and shoved her toward the door. She stumbled and almost fell but regained her footing. Snake followed her out the door.

When mealtime came, the three men ate heartily, seated around a scarred wooden table. The girl huddled near the fire.

"Ain't the little girl havin' any?" Lucius asked.

"You can give her a plate if you want," Cole said, "but *I* ain't payin' for it."

Lucius dished up a plate of beans and laid two pieces of cornbread across it. He gave it to the girl and came back to the table.

Each of the men had a second cup of coffee.

Snake leaned back in his chair and lit a cheroot. "Where you from, boy?" he asked Lucius.

"I come up here from Kentucky."

"You a run-away slave? Maybe got a price on your head?"

"No, suh! Mr. Lincoln freed the slaves. And I served in the Union Army toward the end of the war. So I'm a free man, and this little place is my own."

"Well, don't that beat all," Snake said. "Say, you got any whisky?"

"No, ain't got no whisky. I got some peach wine I made myself. I'll offer that to you. Fifty cents a bottle."

"Well, bring it on," Snake said. He glanced over at Cole, who seemed to be ignoring the conversation.

But as Lucius set the bottle of golden liquid on the

table, Cole muttered, "Hope he's better at makin' wine than he is makin' coffee."

Lucius brought two clean cups, and Snake poured some wine for himself and Cole. After taking a sip, Snake said, "This ain't bad. Kinda sweet. Tastes like peaches alright."

Cole sipped his wine without comment.

"You want me to go put your horses in my shed?" Lucius asked. "I can give'em some hay."

"Sure," Cole said. "What's that gonna cost me?"

"Fifty cents," Lucius said, smiling. He crossed to the door and went out into the night.

Snake drank his wine, seemingly deep in thought. Then he asked, "You really gonna pay him for the food and all?"

Cole snorted. "What do you think?"

"I wouldn't pay a nigger nothin'. We gonna kill him?"

"Can't leave him here to tell about us. You never know, somebody might be on our trail."

"We still takin' that girl all the way to Rockford?"

"Damn right. We'll spread the word in the saloons, and Saturday night we'll have an auction. Sell her off. We might get a couple hundred dollars for her. Some men like'em young — they want to be the first to do'em."

Lucius stood just outside the door, frowning as he listened to their conversation. Then he led the three horses into a lean-to shed next to his own mount. He removed the saddles, tossed the animals some hay, and returned to the cabin.

Cole and Snake ignored him for the rest of the evening, drinking a second bottle of wine. Eventually, after each had taken a turn visiting the outhouse, they spread their bedrolls on the floor and appeared to sleep.

The girl was still sitting on the floor in front of the fireplace. Lucius brought her another blanket. He put down his own bedding and stretched out on the floor, but he did not intend to sleep. After a couple of hours had passed and the other men were snoring, he rose and got his coat and hat and an old .58 caliber Springfield rifle. He moved quietly across the room and slipped out the door without a sound.

Lucius hurried to the shed, saddled his horse, and rode off into the dark forest.

Cole awoke shortly before dawn and realized Lucius was gone. He shook Snake's shoulder until he opened his eyes and started to sit up.

"The nigger's not here," Cole hissed. "Go check outside, see if you can find him."

Snake got to his feet and stumbled toward the door.

"And check the horses while you're out there."

Snake returned in a few minutes, shaking his head. "No sign of him, and his horse is gone. Ours are still there."

"Damn! Something must have spooked him. I figured on lettin' him fix us a good breakfast before we shot him. Wake that girl up and walk her to the outhouse. We need to get out of here. He might bring the law back with him. I'll see if there's any cornbread left and any other food we can take. Go now!"

As light began to show in the eastern sky they were back on the trail.

Another light dusting of snow fell during the night, and the marshal was back on the trail as the first pale colors of sunrise began to glow behind the hills. He could still spot the hoofprints left by the three riders. The fugitives seemed to be moving at the same deliberate pace he was.

He rode until the sun was directly overhead, a hazy, pale orb barely visible through a thick layer of gray clouds. There was little wind, and the surrounding forest was quiet except for the occasional cawing of crows. Once he heard the staccato rapping of a woodpecker. He let his horse drink from a small stream that followed a ravine down from the ridge, and Stone feasted on biscuits and fried bacon Hawkins had wrapped in a piece of oilcloth for him.

After he ate, the marshal traveled for over an hour before he noticed a short path leading off the main trail to a small wooden structure of some sort, perhaps just a shed for storing hay or tools. The rickety building leaned slightly to the left, and the sloping shed roof was covered with moss. Multiple tracks had disturbed the snow in front of the cabin. Stone approached warily, although there was no sign of life around the building. There was a chimney but no smoke, and there were no horses at the hitching post.

He dismounted and tried the door, which opened with a creak. He paused to let his eyes adjust to the dim interior, the only light coming from one small window in the opposite wall. He took another step inside.

Suddenly a thick forearm shot from behind and clamped across his throat. Stone clawed at the arm with both hands, but it was as hard as a length of cordwood. He could not see who was choking him but knew his attacker had to be large. The marshal was big too, yet he was being lifted off the dirt floor. His boot heels kicked and scraped futilely. He could hear the other man grunting softly.

Under the relentless pressure, the marshal felt his eyes bulging and watering, and he began to see flashes of light. He knew it would be only seconds before he lost consciousness. Frantically, he tried again to dislodge the powerful arm, but without success. He squirmed and threw his weight from side to side. Still he could not escape the man's grasp, but his hand fell upon the butt of his pistol. In desperation, he drew the revolver, pointed it down toward the ground behind his own leg, and pulled the trigger.

The roar of the forty-four was deafening inside the small building and was followed immediately by a wild howl. The pressure on his throat was released, and Stone staggered across the room, gasping and coughing. As he began to recover, he turned and saw a huge black man sitting cross-legged on the dirt floor of the shed, holding his right foot in his hands, rocking back and forth, and wailing loudly. The toe of the man's boot was blown open, and blood was oozing from the hole.

"God a'mighty! You shot my toe off!" the man yelled.

"You were choking me to death!" Stone gasped. As the marshal stood, bent, with his hands on his knees, sucking air into his lungs, the black man's wailing gradually subsided to a series of occasional low moans.

"I thought you wuz one of them come back," he muttered.

"Who's that?" the marshal asked. His breathing slowly returning to normal.

"They wuz two men come here last night," the man said, "and I think they wuz outlaws." He gingerly tugged at the edge of the hole in his boot and tried to peer inside at the damage.

"What'd they look like?" Stone asked.

"One — the boss, I'd reckon — wuzn't quite as tall as you. And not quite as old as you neither, but he had some gray in his hair. The other one wuz 'bout as tall, but real skinny. Kind'a nervous actin'. Head like a nickel beer, like my daddy used to say."

"Just the two of them?"

"Naw, they had a young girl with'em. They said they'd pay me for food, so I fed'em. They didn't act like they wuz gonna feed that child at all, so I took her a plate. She wuz cold, so I give her one'a my blankets."

"Did they mistreat her?" Stone asked. "Beat her or have their way with her?"

"No, they didn't do that," the man said. "They shoved her around a little when it was time for her to go to the outhouse, but they mostly didn't pay her no mind. But she wuzn't the kind'a girl that should'a been with men like that at all."

"You're right about that," Stone said. "I don't think either one of them's worth the powder and lead it would take to blow them to hell. They left this morning then?"

"Well, I snuck off in the night 'cause I heard them sayin' they wuz gonna kill me come mornin'. But I watched'em from the woods. They rode off jest before sunup, and I was mighty glad to be shut of'em I can tell you that.

Then, after I come back from runnin' my traps and heard you comin' in the door I thought one of'em had come back to kill me. I'm sorry I tried to choke you."

"Well, I'm sorry I shot you," the marshal said. He moved toward the door. "I've got some supplies in my saddle bags I can use to clean that up and bandage it for you. I'm not a medic, but I did a fair amount of that sort of thing in the war."

At the door, Stone paused and looked back. "By the way, did those men say anything about why they took the girl in the first place — what they plan to do with her?"

The black man took a moment to adjust the position of his injured foot. His eyes remained downcast as he shook his head in disgust and said, "Well, suh,

I overheard the older one say that when they get to Rockford they could sell chances to some'a the men up there. That some would pay to be the first to lay with her. That's when I knew for sure they wuz no good."

Stone just nodded, his expression grim as he went outside. He returned with his medical supplies and cleaned and wrapped the injured man's toe. "Turns out I didn't shoot your toe clean off, just nicked it. Should be fine once it heals," he said. "I'm Marshal Sam Stone, by the way, and I didn't catch your name."

"It's Lucius," the black man answered. "Lucius Poppelwell. Most folks just call me Poppy."

"Well, Poppy, soon as you can, you should get a real doctor to look at that wound. Do you have a horse?"

"Yessuh," he's tied up out back in a little pine thicket."

"Well, you can ride along with me until we get to the next town, if you want. That would be Kirby, and I'm pretty sure there's a doctor there."

"I'd be obliged, marshal. I'll do my best not to slow you down. My cache of hides is well hid, and I can come back for'em in a day or two."

Within a few minutes the two riders were following the narrow road north, toward what the marshal knew could be a violent showdown.

Marshal Sam Stone and Lucius "Poppy" Poppelwell, rode into the town of Kirby. The main street was lined with storefronts, a saloon, a barbershop, general store, and a bank, which was the only brick structure. Stone reined up in front of a saloon, and Poppy pulled up alongside him.

"If you look up there at the end of the street," the marshal said, "there's a livery stable. How about you take the horses on over there while I go into the saloon and find out if our fugitives have been here — or may still be here."

"Fine with me," Poppy said. The marshal handed him a few coins for the livery and then dismounted. Poppy headed down the street with both horses.

The saloon was no makeshift affair — it's focal point was a long walnut bar in front of an elaborately carved back bar which included an ornate mirror and shelves of bottled liquors. Stone looked around for the barkeep, hoping he would be a source of information, but then noticed a commotion at the far end of the long, narrow room.

A small circle of men had gathered around, watching a very large man — obviously drunk — struggling with a young woman who was trying to break free of his grasp.

"Now just settle down there, little lady," the man bellowed. "I figure I've bought enough of this fancy whisky to earn the right to a little bit of your time." He had a tight grip on the young women's wrist and was trying to drag her toward the staircase at the other side of the room.

"We'll just go upstairs for a while, and you'll find I'm a generous fellow," he said, continuing to tug at her.

"That ain't part of my job!" she screamed. "I'm a respectable woman!"

The man laughed. "Not workin' here, you ain't. Now, come on!"

Stone stepped through the ring of onlookers and spoke quietly but firmly. "I don't believe the young lady cares to go with you," he said. "Best let go of her arm and go on about your business."

The man glowered at the marshal and roared, "My business ain't none of your business, you damned old mossback!" Still holding the woman's arm, he tried to pull at her dress with his other hand, and the material ripped to her waist, exposing a breast, shocking even her assailant for a moment. One of the onlookers let out a whoop.

The marshal took a step forward, set himself, and with all the strength he could muster, kicked the big man squarely in the crotch. All the color left the man's face and, with a low keening sound, he dropped to his knees, both hands cupped over his groin. The woman, now freed, cowered next to the wall. She attempted to cover herself, holding the torn dress in place.

Stone drew his pistol and brought the barrel down on the man's head. The bully fell on his face and lay unconscious on the floor.

The marshal turned toward the onlookers, moving his pistol from side to side to cover the room. "Anyone else have something to say?" he asked. No one spoke, and the men quickly moved away, some to the bar and some to various tables where they had left their drinks or a card game.

Stone turned to the woman, removed his overcoat, and placed it around her shoulders. "You shouldn't be here, Miss," he said. "Let me get you somewhere safe." He put his arm across her shoulders and escorted her out of the saloon, pausing for a moment just outside. "What's your name, Miss?"

"Lizzy," she answered, her voice trembling. "Lizzy Taulbee."

"This saloon is no kind of place for you to be working, Lizzy," Stone said. "Are your things in there?"

"Well, I had to have a job," Lizzy said defensively. "My husband died. A tree fell on him. I've only been in town for two days, and my things are still down at the livery stable."

Stone turned and looked up and down the main street of the little town. "I know a few people here," he said. "Would you be interested in a more suitable job that didn't involve fighting off drunks and ruffians?"

"Oh, I surely would!" she agreed, pulling the marshal's overcoat more tightly around her.

"Why don't you go over to the livery stable, put on a better dress, and then meet me at the dry goods store over there?"

Her eyes brightened. "Oh, yes, I will." She started in that direction, then turned and said, "Thank you, marshal. I don't know what would have happened if you hadn't been there."

"Just doing my job," he said.

Stone sat on a public bench near the dry goods store and smoked a cigar until Lizzy appeared again. She came hurrying along the street in a light blue cotton dress with a white lace collar. Stone had to admit she was an unusually attractive young lady. She had a heavy shawl around her, and she returned the marshal's coat to him.

He held the door for her and they approached the counter inside the store. Stone always enjoyed the smell of cloth and leather and new denim that permeated the shop. The aroma of fresh ground coffee added to the appeal. A tall, thin man wearing spectacles stood behind the counter.

"Marshal Stone," he said. "How nice to see you."

Stone shook the man's hand. "Good to be here," he said. "Hope you and the missus have been well."

"We have indeed," the man said, smiling. As his gaze shifted to Lizzy, the marshal said, "Lizzy Taulbee, I'd like you to meet Harold Godby, the proprietor of this fine establishment."

"Nice to meet you, young lady," Godby responded.

"A pleasure to meet you, sir," Lizzy said.

"And that brings us to the reason for our visit," Stone explained. "Mrs. Taulbee recently lost her husband to a logging accident, and she is in need of honest employment. I was hoping you might find a place for her in your shop."

"Oh, my," Godby said. "I wish I could help, but we have not been busy enough of late to justify taking on another employee. I'm afraid my wife would wring my neck if I were to take on someone new." His expression indicated he was truly sorry. Then he tapped his chin with his forefinger as if entertaining a different thought. "Can you cook, Mrs. Taulbee?"

"Why, yes, I can cook," Lizzy answered. "Nothing fancy, but plenty of good wholesome food — meat and potatoes — and pies. Back home I'm known for my pies."

Godby smiled brightly. "Well, Mr. and Mrs. Frysinger, who own the café, recently lost their cook — she moved to Rockford. I think they would be happy to see you, and they are good, decent people. They also have living quarters for their cook in the back of the restaurant, I believe."

"Mr. Godby, we can't thank you enough!" Stone said, shaking the storekeeper's hand again. "We'll go speak to them right now."

"Thank you, sir," Lizzy added.

They hurried down the street to the Cozy Corner Café, where they met Mr. and Mrs. Frysinger, and within an hour Lizzy had not only a new position as their cook but also a tidy room in the back of the store.

As they walked back into the street they saw Poppy approaching from the livery stable.

"Miss Taulbee, this is Lucius Poppelwell, also known as Poppy. He's traveling with me temporarily."

"How do you do, Mr. Poppy?" she responded.

"Generally I do pretty good until someone shoots my toe off," he grinned.

Stone explained that he had assisted Lizzy in getting a job at the cafe as well as a place to stay in the back of the building.

"We need to get you over to the doc so he can see to that toe," Stone told him. They all said their goodbyes, and Stone and Poppy headed back down the street.

The doctor's office was on the second floor of the hardware store and was reached by wooden stairs on the side of the building. As Stone entered, the white-haired physician was sitting at his desk. He rose and gave a nod of welcome. "Marshal," he said.

Stone took Poppy's arm and pulled him into the room. The doctor raised his eyebrows when he saw the big black man but said nothing.

"This is Mr. Poppelwell," Stone said. "We had kind of a misunderstanding, and I shot him in the toe. Since I felt more or less responsible, I thought he should have it looked at."

"Humph!" With a weak wave of his hand, the old doctor indicated Poppy should sit on a nearby chair. He had him pull off his boot and sock and then removed the bandage Stone had applied.

"You're lucky," he said. "The bullet didn't take your toe clean off — just a piece of it. I'll clean the wound up again and put on a fresh bandage. It should heal up alright."

Once the doctor's work was done, Stone gave him a dollar and he and Poppy went outside.

"I'm going to keep heading north," Stone said, "try to catch up with those killers."

"I'll go with you if you want," Poppy said. "I ain't forgot those men planned to kill me."

"I've appreciated the company," Stone said, "but this isn't your fight. Those men have to answer for what they did to the Hostettler family. Maybe I'll see you on the way back."

He shook the big man's hand, turned, and headed toward the livery stable.

When Cole, Sneed, and the girl rode into Rockford, Cole immediately spotted a storefront that appeared to be abandoned. A faded sign that read "Hardware" had come loose on one end and hung crookedly over the door. The windows were made opaque by a thick layer of dust. It appeared lifeless.

The trio went around the corner and into an alley, stopping at the rear door of the building.

"Go in and make sure there's no one in there," Cole told Sneed. The door was locked, but Sneed had little trouble jerking it open. He disappeared inside and returned a few minutes later.

"Nobody there. Looks like it's been out of business for a long time. Lot of junk in there, but the third floor's wide open, like a big ballroom or somethin'."

"Well, if it was a hardware store, there should be some rope around," Cole mused. "Take the girl up to that third floor and tie her up. Then we'll check out the saloons, see where we might auction her off."

Sneed took the girl inside, and Cole dismounted

and tied the horses at a hitching rail behind the next building along the alley. As he started to turn back, the cold barrel of a pistol was shoved against his neck.

"Hold it, mister!" a man's voice barked. "Very slowly take that pistol off your belt and drop it. Then put your hands up."

Cole did as the man said. Then he asked, "Who are you, and what do you want?"

"I'm the town marshal here," the man said. "I was warned to be watching for two men with a young girl that might be headed here. And I'm wondering if that may be you. Who do the other two horses belong to?"

"Do you mind if I turn around?" Cole asked.

"I've got my pistol on you. Don't try anything," the lawman said.

Cole turned and saw that the marshal was a much older, white haired gentleman with a bushy white mustache. A brass badge was pinned to his vest. The pistol he was holding was old and worn but appeared well oiled.

"Who warned you about these people you're looking for?" Cole asked.

"The district marshal, Sam Stone, sent a telegram to the station in Seymour, and a messenger brought it out here. Now you answer *my* questions. Who rode in on those other two horses?"

"Well," Cole began, "my associate, Mr. Sneed —"

Now the marshal felt cold steel against the back of *his* neck and heard the click of a hammer being cocked.

"And here is Mr. Sneed now," Cole said with a cold smile, taking the marshal's gun. "What do you say we all go inside to talk, so we don't draw too much attention?"

Inside the abandoned store, Cole had Sneed find more rope and tie the town marshal's hands behind him with his back against one of the large posts that held up the room's heavy, rough-hewn overhead beams. Sneed pulled the rope tight so the old man's back was cinched snug against the post.

Sneed walked around in front of the marshal and stood looking him up and down, shaking his head. "Lawman, huh?" he scoffed. He turned as if starting to walk away but suddenly spun around and struck the older man in the stomach, knocking the air out of him. Then he drew back his fist and punched him in the mouth, drawing blood. The marshal gasped for air as blood dripped down his chin.

"That's enough," Cole said. "I want to ask him a few more questions." He walked over and stood in front of the battered man, waiting for his breathing to return to normal.

"Did that district marshal say he was on his way here?" he asked. In response, the old man spat bloody saliva at him.

"So you're a tough old bird, eh?" Cole stepped even closer and drew his Bowie knife. He pressed the sharp point into the soft flesh just below the marshal's jawline, drawing blood. He held the knife there, maintaining the pressure. "I asked if that marshal said he was coming here."

"He didn't say," the old man whispered.

"But he is," Cole said coldly. "And you were supposed to hold us for him, right?" He pressed harder on the knife.

"I reckon." Panic showed in the old man's eyes.

"Who else knows about this?"

"I don't know."

Cole leaned hard on the knife. Blood flowed from the marshal's throat. "Who else knows?"

"Nobody, I swear!"

"What about the telegraph operator?"

"He don't matter. He's clear down in Seymour. I'm the only law here."

"Do you have deputies?"

"No, there's just me."

Cole paused for a moment, pondering the situation, and then plunged the knife deep into the old man's throat. The marshal's body jerked and writhed, and blood gurgled from his mouth. Cole continued to lean on the knife. And then the old man slumped against the ropes and was still.

Night had fallen by the time Stone rode into Rockford. As he walked his horse along the main street, he noticed three burned-out buildings scattered among the surviving businesses, which included a hotel, a couple of restaurants, and at least four saloons — the most brightly lighted establishments, where the sounds of laughter and music spilled into the street.

At the far end of the street stood a small church with clapboard siding that was in need of a fresh coat of white paint.

Stone dismounted in front of the largest of the four saloons and went inside. Behind the bar was a surly man with a scar that ran from his hairline down across his left eye to the corner of his mouth. "What'll you have?" he asked.

"I'm just looking for a little information," Stone replied, moving the lapel of his overcoat to reveal the badge on his vest.

"Well, 'a little' is probably all you're gonna get in *this* town," the man said.

"I'm just asking if you've seen two men traveling with a young girl — very young, thirteen or fourteen maybe."

The man seemed to ponder the information. "The thing is," he said at last, "if someone had a girl that young with'em they wouldn't bring her in here. And if they didn't come in here I wouldn't have seen'em. This place is like my own dark groundhog hole; I don't get out much."

"Seems to me a trio like that might have stirred up some conversation," Stone said. "You sure you haven't even *heard* about anyone like that being in town?"

"I'm afraid I just can't help you, Marshal," he said. "But I'd be pleased to offer you a drink — on the house. Whisky?"

"Maybe another time," Stone said. "Thanks."

As soon as Stone left the saloon, the barkeep signaled to one of four men playing cards at a corner table. The man picked up his cash, his hat, and a Henry rifle and lumbered over to the bar.

The two men conversed quietly for a minute or two, and then the man with the rifle went out into the night.

Stone walked down the street to another saloon, where he was met with a similar stone wall. Neither the bartender nor three customers drinking at the bar would admit to seeing — or even hearing about — two strangers and a young girl. But at a third establishment, a much younger barkeep couldn't hide his nervousness when Stone pressed him for information.

He was a slim young man with blond hair and just the trace of a mustache. His eyes gave him away when the marshal asked him about the men and the girl. After glancing around the room, he said loudly, "I can't tell you anything about that!"

The marshal leaned in closer. With a menacing glare he said quietly, "If you know anything at all, it's best you tell me right now. Those men are killers and kidnappers, and if you withhold information you could go to prison."

"Yeah, but I could get my throat cut too, and you could get your head bashed in," the barkeep whispered. "There's men in this town that want what those two have."

"You mean the girl?"

"The story is they're gonna hold a raffle. Ten dollars a chance. Winner gets to have his way with her, keep her, sell her, do whatever they want with her."

"When is this event supposed to take place?"

"Saturday night. When there's a bigger crowd in town."

"So where are they keeping her in the meantime?"

"If anyone figures out I'm telling you all this I'm a dead man for sure," the young man moaned quietly.

"Why don't you pour me a whisky? You're just serving a customer. Once I get those two it won't matter where I got my information."

The bartender set a glass on the bar and poured the whisky. He raised his voice again. "Look, mister, I don't know what you're talkin' about, alright? Just drink your whisky!"

He pretended to wipe the bar and leaned close. "Go out around to the back alley. I'll go to the back room for somethin' directly and slip out there."

Stone tossed back his drink and left the bar. He walked quickly alongside the building to the dark alley that ran behind it, then waited near the rear door of the saloon. He could hear a player piano in the distance.

After a few minutes the door opened, and the barkeep stuck his head out, saying, "This better be quick!" He stepped outside.

"All I need to know now is where to find them," Stone said.

"Three or four doors down from here there's a hardware store in a three-story building," the young man said. "It went out of business months ago. That's where they're gonna hold the raffle, and that's where they're hiding out."

"Any accomplices with them?"

"Don't think so. Anyway, I gotta get back to the bar." He went back inside.

As Stone turned to leave, a shape loomed out of the darkness and something struck the marshal on the head. The blow staggered him, but he shook it off and started to draw his gun. A second attacker, coming from behind, struck him across the shoulders with a wooden club, and just as Stone's pistol cleared the holster, the first man knocked it away and drove his fist into the marshal's gut. Winded, Stone lashed out wildly and struck the man on the nose. Then he set himself and launched a solid punch to the man's jaw.

Stone turned to face the other attacker just as the man raised the club to strike. The marshal dived against the assailant's chest and drove him hard against the wall of the building. The club fell to the ground. The man swung his fist, but Stone deflected the punch and countered with a sharp uppercut to the chin.

Just as the marshal cocked his arm to deliver a knockout blow, he was blindsided by the first attacker who crashed into him and pulled him to the ground. A second later, the other man threw himself across Stone's legs, pinning them to the ground.

Flat on his back, Stone tried to gain enough leverage to fight back, but the first attacker was now straddling his upper body and delivered a vicious blow to the marshal's jaw. Then another and another. Stone could taste blood, and his strength was fading. He tried to twist his body but could not budge the two heavy men. He was barely able to raise his arms, wearily trying to protect himself from repeated punches. He was starting to lose consciousness. He writhed and struggled desperately, but to no avail.

Suddenly the weight on his legs was gone. Stone heard a muffled cry and a thump, and then the weight on his midsection also vanished. He managed to raise himself slightly on one elbow. He peered through a veil of blood to see a large, dark form that seemed to be holding a man off the ground, and the man's dangling feet were kicking feebly. There was another thump and then silence.

The dark form approached and leaned over the marshal. A face slowly came into focus, and Stone whispered, "Poppy?"

Lizzy Taulbee had just finished her day at the cafe and was looking forward to getting out of her tight shoes and into her nightclothes when she heard a thumping at the door of her room. When she turned the knob, Marshal Stone practically fell into the room, followed closely by Lucius Poppelwell.

"Marshal!" Lizzy exclaimed. "What happened Poppy?"

The big black man half escorted, half carried Stone to the bed in the corner of the room. "Some hooligans in that outlaw town like to beat him to death, that's what happened!" he exclaimed angrily. He began to tug at one of the marshal's boots, and Lizzy crossed the room to help.

"What made you think to bring him here?" she asked.

"Before he passed out, the marshal told me. He said it was the closest that was safe."

"Well, you'd best go get the doc," Lizzy said. "Do you know where that is?"

"Yes'm, I been to his office," Poppy said, heading for the door. "I'll get him."

By the time Poppy returned with the doctor, Lizzy had removed Stone's coat and vest. He seemed barely conscious.

As always, the old physician had the stump of a fat cigar clamped in his teeth as he examined the wounds.

"Well, he's lost some blood, and he's probably got some broken ribs," the doc said. "Likely a concussion, too, but his skull's not fractured, far as I can tell. Gonna be pretty painful for a week or two, but he's a big, strong fellow, and I believe he'll be alright."

"You did well getting him here, Poppy," the doctor said. He turned to Lizzy. "Looks like you get the job of nurse whether you want it or not."

"It's fine," she said. "I'm happy to care for him."

"I'll be back tomorrow to check on him," the doctor said. He turned to Poppy. "Do you have a match?"

Poppy fished in his pocket, pulled out a wooden match and gave it to the doctor who puffed and puffed to get his stub of a cigar lit. The acrid smoke swirled around his head.

"Thanks," the doctor said. "Good night, all. If you need me you know where to find me."

Poppy left with him, and Lizzy found herself alone in the room with the dozing, injured lawman. She adjusted the coverlet up to his chin and then bent over him to kiss him, gently, on the forehead.

At 6:30 the next morning Lizzy had to have hot coffee, biscuits, fried potatoes, steak, ham, bacon, eggs, and flapjacks ready for her customers' breakfasts. After the morning rush she slipped back into her room to find the marshal sitting up in bed, drinking the coffee she had left for him. He was still pale, but his eyes were bright and clear, and he smiled when she entered the room.

"Well, how's our patient today?" Lizzy asked, trying to sound as cheerful as possible. "Ready for some real food?"

Stone smiled. "An egg and some toast might be agreeable," he said. "This coffee has been like a magic elixir — I feel better already."

"Well, you must'nt rush it," Lizzy cautioned. "The doc said you have to care for the physical wound as well as the shock to the system from bein' attacked like that. Both of those things take a lot out of you."

"I'll do what I can," Stone said, "but I don't have a lot of time."

"Time for what?" Lizzy asked.

"What day is this — Thursday?" he asked, and Lizzy nodded. "They're going to auction off that girl on Saturday, and as soon as they get their money they'll be long gone. And Lord only knows what'll happen to the girl. I have to be able to ride by tomorrow — put a stop to it before it happens — come hell or high water."

"Doc's not going to like that," Lizzy said. "You're not going to have your strength back for several days. You won't be completely healed for weeks."

"Unfortunately, I don't have a choice," Stone said. "I need to clean and check my weapons," he added and started to rise but immediately grew dizzy and fell back onto the bed.

"You see?" Lizzy said. She lifted his feet and legs onto the bed and pulled the covers over him. "All you can do for now is rest and try to get stronger. You lie back and take it easy, and I'll go get you that egg and toast — and more coffee. If that doesn't heal you, nothing will!"

The next day, after the noontime rush at the cafe, Lizzy returned to find the marshal standing in the center of the room, trying to put on his frock coat. He was already wearing his shirt, vest, trousers and boots, and the heavy gun belt with the holstered Colt .44.

Lizzy helped him with his sleeve, though her expression was clearly disapproving. "If I didn't know better, I'd think you were going to try to go some-where," she said.

"I have to go, Lizzy," he answered. "It's my job. For one thing, they massacred a family, and there's no way I can let them do what they're planning to do to that girl."

"You may not even make it back to Rockford in the shape you're in," Lizzy said.

"I'll be fine," Stone said. "I've been hurt before; I've been stabbed and beaten, and shot, and left for dead, but I always managed to come back. You'll see."

Suddenly she pulled him to her and kissed him, passionately, on the lips.

"Lizzy —" he started to speak, but she kissed him again with even more heat, pressing her body against him. He could feel the shape and warmth of her through the thin cotton dress she wore.

He placed his hands on her shoulders and held her at arms' length. "Lizzy," he said gently, "this isn't right. You're a beautiful young woman, but I'm old enough to be your father. Hell, I'm old enough to be your *grandfather!*"

He placed his hand on her cheek and smiled. "Don't be in such a hurry. You're a sweet, attractive young lady. You're just getting started here — by spring, decent young men will be swarming around this café like honeybees. And one of them will be the one, and he'll love you, and cherish you and treat you right — just the way you deserve. And I'll be truly happy for you. I will."

"But I feel sad that you live this life that you do and don't have anyone," Lizzy said softly, resting her cheek on his chest.

"Well," Stone said, "truth is, I *do* have someone. And when I finish this last job she'll be waiting for me. So you must'nt worry about me or feel sad for me. I'm looking forward to a new, quiet life with someone I care for. And I want you to have the same."

He kissed the top of her head, picked up his overcoat and hat and headed for the door. "You have a good situation here, Lizzy," he said. "I hope you make the best of it."

And with that he was gone.

Poppy met Stone at the livery stable, and they both saddled up. Once again, darkness was falling as they rode into Rockford. Stone pointed out the abandoned hardware store and the church at the far end of the street where lights in the windows indicated a service was in progress.

"I'll tell you what," Stone said. "You ride on over to that church and tell whoever's there — hopefully there'll be some women — to come over here to the hardware store to help the girl. Tell them what's been happening. Her name's Rosalie, she's only thirteen or fourteen years old, and she's going to need some good Christian women to look after her. Tell'em to come running. I'm going to slip around behind this old hardware store, see if I can get in and get the drop on those killers."

Poppy nodded silently and rode off toward the church. Stone rode immediately to the rear of the store, dismounted and tied his horse to a nearby hitching post. He moved quietly to the rear door and found it unlocked. He slipped into the gloomy interior.

The building was long and narrow, and on one long brick wall he could make out large painted letters stating: "J. A. McKinney Mammoth Store." On the opposite wall, down about a third of the building's length, a wooden staircase led to the second floor.

Stone made his way up the stairs, sticking close to the edge in the hope of minimizing any creaking or other noise from the individual wooden treads. Halfway up, he was overtaken by a sudden weakness, breaking out in a sweat and being forced to lean against the wall for support. His injured ribs were throbbing, and his head felt as if it might explode. After a few moments he felt sufficiently recovered to continue, although his legs seemed weaker than before.

The second-floor room was much like the first — filled with a jumble of dusty merchandise and junk.

At the top of the final flight of stairs was a flimsy wooden door, which he was able to open without a sound. He drew his pistol and stepped into a room very similar to the first floor — long and narrow — but virtually empty. Midway between where he stood and the end wall was a lone wooden rocking chair. On the opposite side, part of the room had been partitioned off and enclosed, probably to create a storage room of some sort.

And at the far end of the room, with his back to the wall, stood Gordon Cole, holding a young girl with blond curls. His left hand was around her waist, and his right hand held the gleaming edge of his Bowie knife against her pale white throat.

Stone took three more steps into the room, and Cole said, "That's far enough, Marshal." The outlaw seemed relatively unconcerned about the situation, speaking casually, as if to an old friend.

"Seems we have ourselves a Mexican standoff," he added. "You'd like to rescue this girl here, but if you try she's gonna end up dead, which won't sit well with the folks back home, right? So we need a plan."

"And what would that be?" Stone asked.

"Well, in its simplest form, you just lay down that revolver of yours, the young lady and I will pass by you and go downstairs, and I will leave her — unharmed — outside and just ride away. I think that's reasonable, don't you?" the killer asked.

"There's one of only two ways you're leaving here," Stone replied. "You can surrender to my custody and throw down that knife and the gun belt you're wearing, or you can be carried out on a board and displayed over at the funeral parlor. It's entirely up to you."

"Now, Marshal," Cole smirked, "you and I both know your record when it comes to rescuing young ladies in this kind of situation isn't very good." He saw Stone's expression darken and continued, "Yeah, I know that story. You couldn't even save your own wife. In fact, the outlaw didn't kill her — *you* did!"

The girl let out a little squeal as Cole pulled her

tighter and pressed the sharp blade even more firmly against her throat.

"You don't want to take another chance on a tragedy like that," the outlaw continued. "Another innocent girl dead because of your incompetence — or is it just your ego that makes you think you can shoot your way out of an encounter like this? Now you follow my plan, nobody gets hurt, and we all live to fight another day. Doesn't that make a lot more sense?"

Stone stood silently for a few seconds. He was feeling lightheaded and swayed almost imperceptibly from side to side. His right hand, which held the cocked pistol, hung loosely at his side.

He looked at Cole's confident, smirking expression, and a sudden calm came over him.

"I've been at this for a long time," the marshal said quietly, "and I've found that some people are so completely evil there's just no place for them in this world."

His cold gaze zeroed in on Cole's face and, after a moment, the outlaw's smirk disappeared, and his eyes widened in fear.

In one fluid motion the marshal raised his pistol, arm fully extended, and fired. The bullet struck Cole in the left eye, and a mist of red exploded behind his head. The knife clattered to the floor, and the girl fell to her knees, her face in her hands, bending forward to the floor, sobbing violently.

The force of the fatal bullet had flung Cole against the wall, and his lifeless body slowly slid down until he appeared to be sitting on the floor with his back against the blood-spattered wall. His upper body and head began to lean to one side. Very little blood trickled from the black hole where his eye had been.

Stone approached the girl and said quietly, "You're safe now, Rosalie. You'll be alright."

He looked around room, quiet now except for an occasional sob from the girl. He crossed to the storage area at the back of the room and opened the door.

From a corner of the small enclosure the man called Snake lunged at Stone with a drawn-out, high-pitched wild scream, holding his pistol with both hands extended at chest height, aimed squarely at the marshal.

Just as Snake fired, Stone's pistol roared, and a bullet stopped the skinny gunfighter's forward motion and ended his inhuman howl. Stone fired again and again. The bullets drove the outlaw back across the room where he crashed into a wall of shelves that came crashing down with a clatter of dishpans, baking tins, and assorted other metal hardware items. Snake lay unmoving amid the debris, bloody rosettes from three closely spaced bullets spreading across his chest.

Stone stood for a moment, assessing the carnage. Then he looked down at his left arm. There was a bullet hole in the sleeve of his coat, and he could feel warm blood running down his arm, soaking his shirtsleeve.

"Aw, hell!" he muttered.

The marshal turned and walked slowly into the open room. He glanced one last time at the lifeless body of Gordon Cole, slumped against the end wall. The girl was still kneeling on the floor, although her sobbing had subsided somewhat. Stone paused beside her. "You're going to be alright," he said softly, placing his hand gently on her shoulder. "People will be coming to look after you." He could, in fact, hear the approaching voices of townspeople coming to help.

The marshal walked slowly toward the center of the room and carefully lowered himself into the rocking chair, leaning back, his legs out straight, boot heels on the floor. His right hand, still holding the pistol, hung loosely over the arm of the chair, the tip of the gun barrel dragging on the floor. His left hand hung limply on the other side, dripping blood.

He thought about Sarah waiting for him at the farm. He thought about Lizzy and Lucius and the many friends and enemies who had crossed his path on the way to this moment. He thought about Willie Hawkins and their final conversation.

"Be content," Willie had said. "That would be my advice."

"Content," the marshal thought. "Content," he whispered, and then he closed his eyes and drifted off to rest.

Author's Notes

✳ ✳ ✳

Because the stories in this collection were written over a period of more than 50 years, there is no continuity of theme or subject matter. Each was written as a separate and independent project.

For example, "The Dreamer" was written when I was still in my teens and reflects a teenager's concerns, while stories such as "Darkroom" and "No Redemption" came several decades later and involve themes of crime and punishment as seen by a writer in his seventies.

Astute readers may notice that "Roller Rink Ruby" employs dialogue that evokes the rhythm of spoken exchanges between actors in a stage production. That is because it was commissioned originally as the script for a proposed musical revue featuring songs from the nineteen-sixties. When plans for the production fell through, I reworked it into short story form while retaining much of the "G rated" dialogue. I'm aware that teenagers of that era were not that innocent or naïve.

While the characters and events in all the stories are fictitious, several are set in locations in the southern Indiana area where I have spent most of my life. If those sites are recognized by any readers, hopefully that will provide some additional enjoyment.

"No Redemption," for example, is my attempt to create a "western" set in southern Indiana in the 1870s rather than in Arizona or New Mexico as is typical of that genre. To establish this location, there are references to some towns that may be recognizable; however, for purposes of the entirely fictional story, the geography of the area and spatial relationships of those communities to one another have been manipulated considerably. It's a story intended to entertain, not to provide an accurate historical record.

Acknowledgements

✳ ✳ ✳

There is no way to adequately express the gratitude owed to my wife, Judy, for her patience, tolerance and encouragement throughout all my creative endeavors. Without her, this book would not exist.

My longtime friend and fellow journalist, John Pesta, himself an award-winning fiction author, and his wife, Maureen, were kind enough to give a first reading to some of these stories, and they provided many helpful suggestions and offered continuous encouragement throughout the process. Their son, Jesse Pesta, a respected journalist in his own right, helped walk me through the process of getting the book into print. And Forrest Willey, a talented photographer with a background in creative writing, provided very helpful suggestions, which were incorporated into "Henry and the Night Sky." He also provided the front cover photograph.

And I must thank all my family —my children and grandchildren, my siblings and their families — for steadfastly supporting all my attempts at art, from photography to music to writing.

And, of course, I owe an immeasurable debt to my parents, the late John and Margaret Persinger, who gifted all their children with an appreciation of the arts and never failed to be excited for our efforts and accomplishments. We miss them every day.